T0090750

Scalpel of Death

Marco Beltran

*We at Trafford believe that it is the responsibility of us all, as both individuals
and corporations, to make choices that are environmentally and socially sound.
You, in turn, are supporting this responsible conduct each time you purchase a
Trafford book, or make use of our publishing services. To find out how you are
helping, please visit www.trafford.com/responsiblepublishing.html*

*Our mission is to efficiently provide the world's finest, most comprehensive
book publishing service, enabling every author to experience success.
To find out how to publish your book, your way, and have it available
worldwide, visit us online at www.trafford.com*

Trafford rev. 8/27/2009

Trafford PUBLISHING®   www.trafford.com

North America & international
toll-free: 1 888 232 4444 (USA & Canada)
phone: 250 383 6864 ♦ fax: 812 355 4082 ♦ email: info@trafford.com

PREFACE

The elegant Lamborghini stopped and turned its lights off.

It had been nighttime for a while, but thanks to the full moon, he was still perfectly able to contemplate the marshland through the windshield of the car. He loved marshlands. They were one of the privileges living in the State of Florida had. There were always marshlands nearby. Those vast swamps that were capable to hide any kind of evidence…

He got out of the car ready to finish with everything once and for all…

He opened the trunk of the car and grabbed the thick plastic bag that had the body inside it. He carried it in his arms and took it nearer to the muddy water.

Before he got rid of the lifeless body, he contemplated the beautiful face of the women long and hard, as if he was hypnotised. Her face was so extremely attractive and delicate, almost perfect. His eyes could not get enough of looking at those delicate features of that face. A face he had created. A face that had been his obsession… What a shame had that mistake been…!

There always were the kind of mistake that destroy something perfect.

After that, his eyes looked at his own hands; which had long and sensitive fingers. The fingers of an artist. Yes! That was what he was, he proudly thought. He was a genius of art, because the purpose of art was precisely that; to highlight beauty. And he had looked for beauty his whole life.

He remembered he had still to do the dirtiest part of the whole business. He went back to the car. He put on the surgical gloves and sighed. He had never liked to get his hands dirty, and he particularly hated to get his hands dirty with blood. He was a careful person and paid attention to details. He had to be like that with a job as his. Then he took an axe out of the depth of the trunk. The blade of the axe shone as he put it on his shoulder. He loved axes as much as his fascination of swamps. He did not only love axes, but also, all types of knives; actually he loved everything that could cut silently and effectively.

Three minutes later, with his body covered in sweat; he threw the body in the swamp. A perverse smile appeared on his mouth as he saw the body sunk deeper and deeper into the dirty water until it finally disappeared.

He did not feel any kind of remorse, or guilt or any kind of repentance. For an artist, those kinds of cheap emotions, those weaknesses of the spirit, were not possible… He thought that the only responsibility of an artist was to perform his art. And he would be ruthless to become the very best of all artists. He had a dream. He is so distressed that he has to get rid of it. He does not feel at easy until he succeeds. The rest does not matter, guilt, sanity, decency, and sometimes even, happiness. Everything has to be sacrificed in order to obtain his perfect work of art…

He returned to the car with the axes and something else in his hands…

He took the surgical gloves soaked in blood off and threw them in the bushes.

He got behind the wheel of his Lamborghini and felt he still was sweating. That was not a good sign, because it would ruin his elegant shirt.

It started to rain. It was a warm and tropical kind of rain.

He drove away in his car and did not think about the woman he just had killed anymore. He was already thinking in another one…

1

"The day has arrived," Laura Duncan thought, while her face was covered in bandage again. She had gone through seven surgeries during the year after the accident. Doctor Vinci had become her saviour and gradually giving her a new face through the art of plastic surgery, trying the transform a nightmare in the beginning of a beautiful dream. She had barely left during this terrible experience; she had remained in her peaceful South Beach home, reading music scores and softly practicing on the piano. She knew she had to pick up her music career eventually. Everyone expected her to do so. The audience, the critics, her close friends. She had started giving concerts when she was eighteen years old and had travelled around the country, from coast to coast, and from north to south. She had never stopped for a long time or cancelled a concert... until the tragedy happened.

She thought about the day of the accident... Even today, when she remembered that day, a shiver went down her spine from her head to her toes. It happened after a convert in Tampa. She was driving her Chrysler back to the south of Florida feeling very tired... The car was going too fast, but she did not notice it, because she was in a hurry to get back home. It was a grey, rainy, but somewhat warm afternoon in February. It was raining so much that the road seemed an ice skating track. Laura saw the abundant rain falling down her windscreen. She could hardly see the road. Then she arrived to a crossroad, but she did not realised she had arrived there. She just felt the impact of the lorry... The Chrysler was the most damaged; it overturned instantly and rolled off the road. A spark was produced in the electric system and after that Laura's head bumped heavily against one of the lateral windows. She was knocked unconscious and the Chrysler began to burn in spite of the rain.

The lorry driver that had caused the accident cowardly drove away from the site.

The flames quickly burned Laura's car, and her hands and her face... Oh! Her face was burned... Fortunately, a police car drove by that place at that exact moment. The police officers saw the fire of Chrysler and immediately helped her. Laura was still unconscious... When she woke up, she was in an hospital bed, sedated and an intense burning sensation in her face, which was almost impossible to bare.

One of the doctors that had attended her said her face and her hands had been burnt in the fire. However, the damage could have been worse; if the police officers had driven by two minutes later than they did, she would have been a horribly roasted piece of meat.

In any case, her burnings were an awful truth. And the worst one was her face. Her delicate and youthful face had been transformed from one minute to the other. Someway or the other, her future and her career as a pianist had been ruined. She had to find a specialist to have her face reconstructed. The best plastic surgeon in the country. Francesco Vinci and his private clinic located in Palm Beach had been recommended to her. That was in the same of Florida were Laura lived....

*   *

Doctor Vinci had finished his surgery on Laura forty-eight hours earlier and was now getting ready to take of the bandages. The change would be spectacular thought the great plastic surgeon. This surgery had been to reconstruct Laura's nose, cheeks and chin. Francesco Vinci felt his pulse rising. This would be his creation...

Laura was also anxious herself. She knew she could face the world again. She would feel alive for the first time this last year... What would the people say? Her always-unconditional audience? The critics? What would her closest friends say?... Would they be surprised? Would they shower her with praise? "My case is not about vanity. No." she said to herself repeatedly. "This is all about reconstructive surgery, plastic surgery for people that have suffered accidents. Desperate people."

"I am going to take of the bandages," Vinci said to her. "Are you ready?"

"Yes doctor," Laura answered.

"Remember that you have to wait for the bruising to go away, especially around your eyes, your cheeks, and your nose." The doctor's voice sounded fine and well educated, but also arrogant and authoritarian. Vinci always made it clear to his patients he was better than they were because of his power and geniality.

"I am anxious to see my new face, doctor," Laura mumbled.

Vinci did not say anything. His elegant and fine hands began removing the bandages. Laura noticed her heart beating violently with the sound of the scissors. It was like a mystery, like an adventure story. She knew that Vinci could not reconstruct her face in such a way she could look exactly the way she looked before the accident. She had seen some pictures on the computer of how the results could be like, but she was anxious to see the real face... in the mirror; in the same mirror that had caused so much pain since the day of the accident.

"How much longer is it?"

"About four minutes," Vinci answered. "Be patient. Everything will be all right.

The minutes seemed to go by very slowly for Laura. It seemed they were the last minutes of her life. They actually would be the first minutes of a new and fabulous period in her twenty-eight years of existence. That was what she hoped anyway. The past year she had alienated herself from her social life and from the stages. Now she would be able to make triumphant comeback.

Vinci kept on taking of the bandages, in silent, meticulously and very concentrated. Laura calmed down a bit and thought that it would have been nice to have shared the moment with a close family member, but there was not any. Her mother had died five years ago. She had never met her father; he had left her and her mother when she had been born. He had disappeared one day and had never come back. He had never heard from him again, although her mother had told her that Jack Duncan was a police officer. Her only sister, Sarah, who had been three years younger than Laura, had died tragically in her adolescence. Sarah, who was a drug addict, was admitted into a health institution to rehabilitate from her addiction. A week after she had been admitted, Sarah suffered a sudden massive heart attack caused by the wrong medicine. Sarah died. Medical negligence was never proven, but Laura and her mother knew that it had happened. From that moment on, Laura did not trust doctors very much... She did not trust doctors until the genius plastic surgeon that was now treating her appeared.

Vinci continued cutting and Laura noticed her hair falling free over her shoulders as the bandages were removed.

"How much longer do I have to wait," she asked again.

"Just one minute, just one minute..." Vinci said.

Oh, this would be so beautiful, so beautiful!

Then, still in complete silence, the doctor took the last bandages off with his supremely elegant hands. Suddenly Laura's brown eyes were revealed. The light bothered her a bit, but she soon became used to it.

She focused her sight on Vinci's handsome face, which had benefited from the services of another talented plastic surgeon. Laura observed Vinci's blue eyes examine her; her mouth, her nose, her cheeks; contemplating every detail, analyzing every stitch. After that, a satisfying smile appeared on the lips of the doctor.

"The result is great!" Vinci said.

Laura also smiled, although every movement of a face muscle hurt very much. She sat on the stretcher and slowly turned her head towards the mirror Vinci had put next to her. The distinguished surgeon thought it was better to let the patient choose the moment they wanted to look. Laura took the mirror a little hesitantly, and after waiting a little, she lifted it and looked at her face. At first, she was a little shocked to see the bruises and the swelling Vinci had warned her about. Nevertheless, she calmed down and studied the details; she started to imagine how her face would look like when her treatment was completed.

"Oh god," she mumbled amazed.

"I suppose that means you are pleased with the results Miss Duncan," Vinci smiled.

"Pleased?" Laura asked. "This is more than I had dreamed." She sighed. She turned towards the surgeon and said: "thanks again, doctor. Thank you very much. You really are a genius…" Then she started crying. Tears of happiness. Of immense gratitude.

Vinci simply nodded. He was accustomed to the fact that women started crying. In such a competitive world as ours, where image and personal appearance are extremely important, beauty is one of the most important resources for women. And no woman likes to lack beauty or what is worse, loose it.

Without saying anything, the doctor left the room, understanding Laura wanted to be alone. Every patient wants to be alone after seeing their new face.

Laura dried her tears while admitting Vinci's work was amazing, almost miraculous… Her face was now perfect, just as the surgeon had promised her. That man was really an artist, a sculptor that worked with flesh, bones and cartilage. He was someone that could create absolutely new person with the best of the futures. She slightly tilted her head to one side and looked in the mirror again, from a different angle this time.

"Hi there gorgeous", she whispered, feeling ashamed about her outspoken vanity. She laughed but the pain she felt of her skin made her stop immediately.

*   *

Vinci left the room where Laura was with her new face and went to his office on the fifth floor of the clinic. Feeling full of conceit and arrogance, he sat at his oak desk and opened Laura Duncan's file. He took a sketch he had made of the face the patient would have after the surgery. Was his work similar to the sketch? He analyzed the sketch with his expert eyes for a long time.

"Beautiful," was his conclusion. "An authentic piece of art." After that, he started to talk alone in his office as he used to do. "I think we did it," he went on, smiling now while he looked at the sketch and some photographs of Laura before the last surgery. At the back of the sketch, he wrote 'May – Miami'. He put it back in the file again and locked it away.

He pushed the button on the intercom and told his secretary that he did not want to be disturbed for at least a few hours. He would work on a videotape. He always used the television to give testimony of the results of his experiments. He had even created a series of videotapes with a complete plastic surgery course in different languages that were destined to medicine students and plastic surgeons in the rest of the world.

He got up of his chair and opened the door that lead to the back of the office. He went into this new room. It was a private television studio for his use exclusively. He knew how to use the equipment and he was used to record videotapes without any help. He just stood in the area delimited in front of one camera.

He turned the lights on. He locked the door. He did not worry about being heard, because the studio was completely soundproof. He suddenly felt very tired. However, he knew it was not simply tiredness but it was emotion. It usually happened after her took off the bandages of a face he had created. He opened a drawer in the wall and opened it with a key. He inhaled a stripe of the magic dust. The cocaine made him immediately feel vital and confident again.

He carefully combed his thick dark hair and straightened his tie. He was obsessive about his personal appearance. He started the recorder and stood in front of the camera.

"Ladies and gentlemen," he started saying with that charming voice, although full of arrogance and authoritarian which was common of an egocentric and ambitious person. "You already know me. I am doctor Vinci and I want to inform you that today is a great day for Arts and for the Science of Plastic Surgery. I want to inform you about some actions that I have performed to be able to obtain complete perfection. But before that, I want you to know that what I am about to tell you goes beyond good or evil, beyond sanity and ethics..." he hesitated for a moment before he continued. "Ladies and gentlemen, I want to tell you about a medical miracle. Her name is Laura Duncan, and I fell able to predict that her face, completely created by me, will be the face of the twenty first century. She will probably appear on the covers of magazines and in movies. Her perfect face, the face of a Greek princess will be idolized and adored by western people like they worshipped legendary faces of the big screen like Monroe or Garbo... I have proven that the work of a plastic surgeon is equivalent to the work of geniuses of the Italian Renaissance: Michael Angelo, Botticelli, Raphael... and I have immortalized a face.

*   *

At the same moment Vinci was in front of the cameras, a sixty-year-old man nervously walked around the gardens of the famous plastic surgeon's clinic. He occasionally looked at Vinci's office. There seemed to be anxiety in his look. It was as if he knew that inside the clinic was the answer to some deep, and extremely personal, secret.

*   *

Vinci went to see Laura at night. She had no idea of the plans he had for her. And he knew it was too early to tell her. Vinci actually wanted Laura to embrace fame slowly.

He went in her room very elegantly dressed in a red robe, similar to the one worn by cardinals. He greeted her with an enormous smile on his face and walked towards her bed.

"How do you feel?" he asked her.

"Fantastically," Laura answered. "My face just feels a bit rough... But I can't get enough of looking at myself in the mirror... It is really a miracle, doctor. Thank you very much."

"I am glad that you are happy, Miss Duncan," Vinci said, while he touched Laura's new features with his sensitive hands. He immediately answered: "the roughness of the skin will last for a while. Like I had told you before, we can anticipate the way the epidermis will heal of a patient that has suffered previous burnings and also because of the proteinic levels of each person's skin. Your skin is genetically fabulous. I can guarantee that you will have a marvellous recovery, and you will look great at the end." He stopped talking for a little while. "Can I take the bandages off your hands now?"

"Yes," she answered.

Vinci's blessed hands cautiously took of the bandages with some scissors, just as he had done hours before. Laura was not feeling as anxious to see the result of her hands, although she knew that the healing would be more slowly than that of her face, because the hands were tools that never rested.

Vinci took off the last bandage and ordered:

"Move your fingers... very carefully."

Laura did. She instantly felt the tightness of the skin again.

"When do you think I will be able to play the piano normally again?" she asked.

"In about three months, maybe more," Vinci answered. "That will depend on the care you have of your hands. You have to promise me you will only move your hands the least as possible in order not to force the ligaments.

"I promise, doctor."

"I also want you to see something," Vinci went on talking. "Something that will be a bit tough, but necessary."

"What is it about?"

"You will know in a minute."

Vinci opened the door of the room and gave an order to someone. A table on wheels with a computer on top of it was placed in front of Laura's bed, who was looking at the black screen in interest. Vinci turned the computer on. There immediately appeared an image of Laura on the left side of the screen. She mad a annoyed gesture with her face and looked to another side.

"I know it is difficult to see how one was before."

Laura looked at the screen again for a second, and observed her horribly burnt face, as well as the wounds on her damaged cheeks and her broken nose. It was a horrible sight.

"That was the most horrible thing that could ever happen to a person," she mumbled. She remembered that many time she thought that only suicide would be the solution to all her problems. The only that had kept her from jumping out of the window of the room was her faith in Vinci.

"Now observe this," the doctor continued. He wrote something on the keyboard and created a drawing on the left of the screen; 'the new face' he had shown Laura before the surgery.

Then Laura carefully analysed the screen, amazed about such a modern technological display and then looked at herself in the mirror. The 'new face' drawn on the computer screen and her current face were exceptionally similar.

"Unbelievable," she exclaimed.

"It may well be that we will have to work a little more on some details," Vinci said, always with arrogance. "Some little details. That is very common."

"Whatever you say," Laura answered, still observing the drawing and still amazed by what had been created with her burnt flesh and broken bones.

"I do not think we have to change any of the basic features," the surgeon continued. "I hope you agree with me."

"Oh yes, of course I do."

Vinci took out a note pad and a pen.

"I am going to prescribe some medicine to you," he said while he wrote on the paper. "It will help in your recovery and it will reduce part of the tightness... And I think it will be useful that you had some session with a therapist."

"A psychiatrist?" Laura was surprised.

"That would be convenient."

"Why? Is something wrong with me?"

"No. I advise this in an eighty percent of the cases. You will go back to work and you will go through a period of transition to fit back into the external world, and part of this period could be quite difficult. And if that should be the case, a therapist would really help you."

Laura looked at him. She had never been to a psychiatrist before. She did not like them very much; she related them to madness, identity loss and being

emotionally weak. And nobody likes to fell they are loosing their mind. She blinked for a few seconds and said:

"I am sure I can handle this on my own."

"Of course you can," Vinci agreed categorically. Bu you should remember that the world of attractive people is not the same as the world of not attractive people. After your accident, you belonged to the latter and now after the surgery you will belong to the former. The way we look affects our capacity to adapt. You will do well in life because you are attractive again. However, you probably will still feel unattractive for a while. I recommend you have some counselling."

The reasons Vinci was giving were very reasonable and seemed backed up Laura thought. It seemed impossible to go against a prodigious brain as that of Vinci.

"Alright, I will do it," she resigned. "I had never imagined that they were two completely different worlds," she said.

"I know, but they are," the surgeon continued. "I will tell about a fact I discovered personally some years ago, after treating some prisoners in a prison in Florida... I discovered that the unattractive prisoners had a greater change of committing crimes again than the attractive ones. I have been working with prisoners for years correcting genetic malformations on their faces, burnings, and scares produced by beatings. The prisoners are less aggressive after the surgery, because everybody looks at them les suspiciously." The doctor stooped talking for a minute. Then he went on: "my experience in orphanages is similar. The beautiful and healthy children are happier than those that are not. I have correct many bone and cartilage malformations through plastic surgery." He nodded and concluded: "the way a person looks can destroy him or her. And yes, there are two completely different worlds; one of the attractive people and one of the people that are not attractive."

Laura was fascinated by the fact that the best plastic surgeon in the world, the man that was surrounded by multimillionaires and famous people, had worked in prisons and orphanages.

Vinci suggested an excellent psychiatrist, who had done post degrees Australia and whose office was located in Biscayne Boulevard, next to the South Beach area here Laura lived.

*   *

Francesco Vinci went out of Laura's room, leaving her lying on the bed, without imagining that the elderly man was still waiting outside the clinic. Nobody worried about him. It was usual to see people waiting outside hospitals and health institutions.

*   *

2

Laura was reading a magazine when somebody knocked on the door. She looked up towards the entrance of the room. Somebody with a big and warm smile came in.

"Larry! How nice to see you!"

Laura really meant it. Larry Wallace was very dear to her. The man that had just come to visit her was her friend, her lover and her artistic and publicity manager. He was almost twenty years older than she was, but Laura thought he was charming and good. Besides being her manager, Larry worked for the Miami Globe newspaper.

"I can not believe it, Laura..." Wallace said very surprised. "You look gorgeous... It is really unbelievable."

"Thank you."

"I suppose this is the great surgeon Mister Vinci's the work," he assumed.

Laura could sense some irony and annoyance in Wallace's words. Wallace was definitely jealous of the doctor. Sometimes her friend behaved very compulsively jealous because of the age difference that existed between them. He saw a possible competitor for Laura's love in each young man she knew.

"You are not jealous of Vinci, are you?" Laura asked.

Larry hesitated but did not answer. He opened his leather jacket. After that a present appeared in his had; a round box wrapped in golden paper. He gave it to Laura. He sat down on a chair and asked her:

"Have your friends seen yet?"

"Larry, you are the first to see me."

"I am glad," Wallace said. "I always wanted to be the first!" he joked around. "And you know that."

Laura unwrapped her gift.

"Cognac bonbons. How delicious!"

"They are your favourite bonbons, aren't they?" he said.

They kissed. Then Laura remembered something and confessed:

"Larry, I wanted to thank you. Well, you know what I am talking about right?"

"Thank me? For not leaving you after the accident..."

"Yes," she sighed. "At that moment my career as a pianist was destroyed as was my face... Nevertheless, you... You were the only one that supported me through it all. You gave me the confidence I had lost myself. You and doctor Vinci..."

"There, you mentioned the guy again," Wallace interrupted her.

"I have to," Laura assured him. "He gave me back my life."

"I already know that the guy is brilliant, attractive, and seductive," Wallace said. "Everybody say the same." He ate a mint. "I do not want him near you, honey."

Laura looked strangely at him.

"Why are you saying that?"

Wallace leant on the chair.

"What do you know about him, Laura?"

"I do not really know very much about him," Laura answered while she reflected on the topic. "I have been with Vinci more time than I have been with any other man in my life. He has made a greater impact on my life than any other man as well. Still we do not talk about anything else than medical problems. What I am trying to say, is that he knows my history. It is on my clinical report. But I think that as a patient, I do not ask him about his story." She put the pillow behind her back. "Tell me what you know about Vinci, Larry."

"Well, as a journalist, I have heard some things related to that plastic surgeon," he started saying. "They are not very flattering things. And they have to do with his past."

"Tell me."

"Not yet, honey. First, I have to corroborate my sources. I will tell you later." He decided to change the topic. "When do you think you could start your concerts again?"

"I do not know," she answered disappointed. "The finger's ligaments have to heal. If I move my fingers too much, the pain will come back. The doctor estimates that in three months or so every kind of pain will have disappeared."

"Alright," Wallace said. "I will cancel the concerts for the following six months. Is that alright with you?"

"Excellent."

"Your audience and the critics will want to know about you. What are you going to tell them?"

"I do not really want to know anything about the audience and the critics yet," Laura answered. "Do you understand me?"

"Of course I do, sweetie."

They kissed again. Suddenly, a nurse came into the room. She gave Laura a sedative. Laura soon felt very sleepy. Laura very politely said goodbye to Larry, and Larry said he would come back to visit her the next day. Then he left the room.

Laura felt asleep while she thought that those two men were part of her life now. One of them was a great surgeon that wanted to transform her into a big international celebrity. The other one was her friend, partner, and lover who said that he loved her with all his heart.

* *

Larry Wallace left Vinci's clinic at night. When he left, he noticed a sixty or so year old man curiously looking at him. The man did not come near him, nor did he attempt to follow him. He just looked at Larry, as if he was expected something from him.

As Larry turned his back towards the man, he did not notice that he took his wallet out of his pocket and looked at a photograph in it. The old man looked at it in silence for some time; with eyes full of tenderness and nostalgia. A face made him smile happily.

That face was everything in that man's life.

*   *

Vinci went to see Laura again before noon. On this occasion, two very elegant women accompanied him around forty years both. One of them was a famous women's hairdresser from Hollywood. The other one was an also very well known designer. After introducing both women to Laura, Vinci said:

"Miss Duncan, I always help my favourite patients even in the most personal details. These women, madam Chantal Dumas, and madam Sofia Manzini are going to take care of you. Madam Dumas will do your hair according to my indications; and madam Manzini will dress you from head to toes also according my orders. Form now on, Miss Duncan, you will be a frequent client of these two experts." He smiled while he ordered the collar of his shirt. "And you do not have to worry about the expenses; I will pay for everything. Ok, let's start working."

Madam Dumas, together with some of her assistants, lasted around one hour and a half to do Laura's hair. Laura had to admit the result was excellent. After that, it was the turn of the designer, who dressed Laura is some very fine garments.

Laura felt fascinated. She had become the modern Cinderella, and she had to admit that all the attention she was receiving was great. She had always to be pampered and cared about, because she had not been able to experience that after her father left and her mother died. What else could she possibly ask for in her life? It looked like her future was going to be splendorous... Nothing could go wrong...

*   *

The old man was still waiting outside the clinic. He occasionally looked at the photograph in his wallet. It was the photograph of a young woman with long and thick brown hair.

But, where was she? Where was that person he so desperately wanted to see? Why did she not come out the door of Vinci's clinic?

Who was trying to avoid all of this? Why? Why would anyone do such a thing?

*   *

While Laura was receiving all kinds of special treatments, Vinci left his new creation and went back to his office. He had to make a very important phone call that was essential for his career. He made the phone call himself without the intervention of any of his secretaries. He had memorised the number, because he did not want it to be written on some piece paper.

The phone on the other side of the line rang several times before a female voice answered. The voice seemed tired and somewhat drunk.

"Scylla?" Vinci asked.

"This is her," the female voice answered. "Who is this?"

"This is doctor Francesco Vinci."

"Oh yes. How are you doc?"

Scylla drank some more bourbon, and then she let herself fall on her old and worn out bed. It was the same bed in which many men of New Orleans had had sex with her in exchange of money. That was life of someone that enjoyed sex and the desires of the flesh twenty-four hours a day. Sex, alcohol, and dancing some hours in a deplorable nightclub in the French Quarter were her life. Scylla ran her fingers through her messy and dirty hair. Her hair was almost as dirty as the red dress she was wearing. The most flamboyant were her huge sunglasses that were hiding most of her face. Her face could have been a very attractive one, if it had not been for the scar on one of her cheeks. It had not healed correctly on that face after a plastic reconstructive surgery.

"How are you feeling, Scylla?" Vinci asked.

"Not very good…" the female voice answered. "Since my face was screwed up… I have not been able to look myself in the mirror… Why had you not call me doctor? You know I like to hear your voice…"

"I am calling you now, am I not?" Vinci said. "I am calling to tell you that I going to travel in New Orleans in some days. I will examine that horrible scare."

"The only thing I want is to make the scar on my cheek disappear," Scylla said. "Why did this happen to my face, doc? Why?"

Vinci had thought that surgery had gone all right, until the scars had appeared around the stitches.

"I do not really know," the doctor said. "Something must have happened after the surgery. Maybe we took the bandages off too soon." He stopped talking for a moment.

"But do not worry; I will fix all of this. Just trust me. I already transformed your face once. I can do it again."

"All right, doc. Then I will wait for you here," Scylla drank the rest of the bourbon.

"Yes, yes," the doctor said. "Do not drink too much, and do not meet with bumps," he advised her. Then he hung up.

Scylla Dubois also hung up the phone in Louisiana.

*   *

3

Larry Wallace visited Laura almost every day, and every time he took a box of cognac bonbons.

Two days before Laura was going to leave the famous clinic in Palm Beach, the journalist and artistic manager of the young woman came around her room again.

"Excuse me miss," Larry burst into the room, walking and talking like an old man. "Reverend Wallace is visiting his sick parishioners…"

"Hi, dear," Laura smiled. She remembered that Larry's father had been a parish priest of a catholic community in Boston.

Larry also smiled. He opened his leather jacket. He took out two beautiful orchids

"What beautiful flowers!" Laura said while she took the flowers. "What a good idea to change the bonbons for flowers. I was getting tired of all that chocolate."

"The important thing is that you do not get tired of me…" the journalist joked around.

"No, no, Larry. That will never happen."

Wallace raised one of his brows.

"Nice hairdo," he said. "A bit extravagant, but nice."

"Another gift from doctor Vinci," Laura said. "You should my new dresses, you would simply die. The famous Sofia Manzini has designed them. What do you think?"

Wallace wrinkled his forehead before he answered. He sighed and ate another mint candy. After that, he said:

"You are really impressed by the charming Francesco Vinci, the greatest plastic surgeon of the planet."

"He is a great doctor, without any doubt in my mind," Laura said enfatically.

"Yes, that is true," Wallace, admitted. "But there are a lot of other things too. If you only knew what I found out about him."

Laura pushed the button that lifted the back of her bed. When she finally was sitting straight, she winked and looked at the journalist.

"Tell me everything," she mumbled.

Wallace took a piece of paper from the pocket inside his leather jacket.

"We are not talking about a brilliant that went to medical school, studied hard, and made his parents proud of his career... The guy has a dark past." Wallace started to read the piece of paper. "His real name is John Gravani and he grew up in New York, and not precisely in a very good neighbourhood. His father was a house painter."

"A house painter?" Laura said surprised. "A house painter? There is nothing wrong with being a house painter; but God, the way he talks and his modals; I thought was member of some Italian aristocratic family."

"Well that is incorrect," Larry replied. "He studied all those years with the help of grants. And his first jobs were as a portrait drawer and street photographer in Central Park."

"Are you kidding?"

"No I am not honey. None of the art schools accepted him. They though his work was terrible and had no quality. Finally, he entered an academy in Baltimore, but he did not finish. He was expelled from the academy because of indecent and unethical behaviour. After that, he went to South America where he became involved with drug dealers who sent cocaine to the West Coast of the United States. Larry stopped talking for a moment. "He probably has contact with the New York mafia."

Laura could still not believe what she was hearing.

"But how was he able to graduate as a surgeon with that background."

"I will tell he managed to do that," Larry answered. "After he came back from South America, he spent some time in the army, in the special forces. How did he get in the army? That is a mystery... But from there he entered a programme and studied medicine for six years; you know two years of preparation and four years of medical studies."

Laura said:

"I am surprised he entered the army after being expelled form the art academy and having connections with drug dealing and the mafia."

"He never mentioned them to anyone. He simply lied."

"And the man was involved a real criminal situation," Wallace said. "One night, as he was out partying with some friends, he beat up a prostitute so badly, he almost killed her..."

"And that is the man who has his hands insured for more than three million dollars," Laura said disconcerted.

"Because of that incident, he was arrested and spent more than a year on probation. In addition, he was suspended from medical school for a while. Nevertheless, he finally graduated with mediocre grades. He performed his professional training period in South America: in Brazil and Venezuela. After that, he started to work... That is all that I have been able to find out about him. I have not been able to find out how he became so famous and why he is used to living the life of a prince."

Laura reflected in silence for a moment. Then she answered Wallace:

"But how could he hide everything?"

"Hide what?"

"None of this has ever been publicly known."

Wallace wrinkled his forehead again.

"Nobody investigated anything," he answered. "Nobody made any questions. In Vinci's office, or to be more correct, Gravani's office, they just give the normal and usual facts about his life. They said he lived in New York, that he studied in John Hopkins, and that he is the most famous plastic surgeon in the world and that he has performed some amazing surgeries in famous and rich people...The art academy is not here, the army is not here either. The arrest is not mentioned... Look, nobody here has ever had any reason to question the guy's background."

"And neither do we," Laura said. "Larry, what you have just told me is fascinating, but guy is still a great doctor. You have to admit that."

"Of course," Wallace admitted. "That is what makes the guy so incredible fascinating." Then Larry started to mention some of the ostentatious likes the great surgeon had; autumns spent in Paris and Venice; summers in the Bahamas and Las Vegas.

At that exact moment, somebody knocked at the door. Laura recognized the way of knocking and made a gesture to Larry, who stopped talking.

"Come in."

The door slowly opened. Francesco Vinci, whose birth name was John Gravani; the son of a poor house painter, came into the room wearing an extremely elegant white suit, a Cartier watch on his left wrist and a black tie with a diamond in the middle of it. He acted very vainly and sure of himself, but at the same paternal.

"Oh," the great surgeon said. "I did not know you had visitor, Miss Duncan."

"Doctor Vinci," Laura answered; "I would like to introduce you to Larry Wallace, my artistic and publicity manager and journalist at the Miami Globe."

Wallace noticed a sparkle of jealousy in Vinci's light eyes. Undoubtedly, the distinguished doctor did not like journalists. They were professionals whose work was precisely to stick their noses in other people's business, sniffing around people's past. The same past Vinci was determined to keep secret. Despite this, she shook hands with Laura's friend.

"It is nice to meet you, Mister Wallace," Vinci mumbled. Then he looked at Laura. "I just came to see how you were doing, Miss Duncan. I see you are doing excellently well... All right, I think I will come back later."

"I should be he one to leave..." Larry started to mutter.

"No, no, that is definitely not necessary," Vinci replied emphatically. "You should stay with Laura, Mister Wallace. She needs to start to relate with the outside world. I am to one leaving. I have a lot of work to do in my office." At that exact moment, Vinci said goodbye to both, turned around and left the room.

*   *

"My new face is recovering extremely well," Vinci said talking to the camera in the television studio. He was holding two recent photographs of Laura, which he was showing in front of the camera. He cleared his throat and continued: "I intend to reach absolute perfection... if everything goes without any inconvenience... Laura Duncan is an excellent patient. She is perfect for my objective.

I do not think she knows is part of my experiment. Like the previous patient, she is too in love with her new face that she is not thinking about anything else. But it is very important that you, plastic surgeons of the future, know all the details of what has been done..."

He stopped talking for a moment. It was necessary to inhale some more of magic dust, of course far away of the camera. Then he went back in front of the camera.

"I have embarked on a project to create the female face of the twenty first century," he continued talking. "The perfect face, the face of a new period in the history of humankind. The face that will produce great enthusiasm in the world and will probably become a legend... I have developed innumerable researches to determine exactly how this face should be like... How does one reach real perfection?... What percentage of failure can one foresee?" he took out another photograph from one of the drawers of a desk and held it in front of the camera. " I will give you some answers..."

*   *

The man with grey hair that was standing outside the clinic was becoming visibly tired. He had been waiting to see that face that would bring back serenity back to him, from the early morning until the dark night. He was wondering ow much longer he would have to wait. Maybe the woman he was looking for would never come through those doors...Or maybe she would.

He lit another cigarette and continued waiting.

He had not lost his hopes yet. It was the hope that kept him alive.

*   *

4

Vinci discharged Laura on a beautiful morning in spring. It was the perfect time, because the cool wind had disappeared in the South of Florida, avoiding possibility of pain caused to the new skin of Laura's face. The cool wind and low temperatures were the worst enemies of surgically treated face. This is what cinic used to say.

On that occasion Larry Wallace, her partner was not out of town on some work for the newspaper, so there was nobody to accompany back to her peaceful house in South beach, just next to the Flamingo Park.

When Laura walked through those smoked crystal doors of the clinic, holding her suitcase, she did not notice the presence of the older man standing opposite the building while he smoked a cigarette. She did not notice the impact her new face produced in the man. Laura was just concentrated on getting home.

She stopped a taxi. She got into it and gave her address.

During the ride home, her mind filled up with images. The more powerful ones were of Francesco Vinci's face. Was everything Larry had told her true? It seemed incredible that that man was a … fraud.

Then Laura thought, she would start studying her music immediately; Bach, Chopin, Brahms, Couperin, Hayden and Mozart. She had neglected them too long; the same way she had neglected the piano. She would back to playing piano, although she would be careful not to excessively move the ligaments of her finders.

She arrived to her house. She paid the driver and got out of the taxi.

Suddenly, another car stopped next to her. The back door of the car opened violently. A tall man with grey hair and around sixty years old appeared.

Laura recognised him now. It was the man that had been outside the clinic when she had left.

"Do not run away! Oh god!" he screamed at Laura. "Wait, you are my daughter...!"

Laura stopped feeling very surprised, almost paralysed, looking fixedly at the mature ma, asking herself if he could be her father that had come back after thirty years without knowing anything about him. Maybe he had finally come back to her... Could that be possible? Or maybe was he somebody else...

"Nora," he shouted. "My Nora!" He embraced her strongly, almost crying. "Nora, my baby, my girl! Where had you gone? Why did you leave us? Your mother...? Did you know about your mother...?"

Laura was astonished. She did not how to react...

Nora, talk to me!" the man anxiously shouted at her. "I have been waiting for more than a year. I waited outside that clinic. I knew you would go back there."

At that moment, Laura understood it was all a terrible misunderstanding. She stepped away from the man.

"Sir," she said slowly. "I am afraid there has been a misunderstanding. Please, sir..."

"Please!" the man begged. "You are my Nora. Don't play tricks with me!"

"I am not playing tricks with me," she said. "My name is Laura Duncan.

"No, no, no," the man insisted. "Do you think I would not recognise my own daughter? Why are you doing this, Nora?"

"I am not Nora," Laura said as she took the porch's key and stormed in, followed closely by the man. She almost told the stranger to go away. To leave her alone; but she decide to talk to him. She invited him to sit on one of the beach chairs in the porch.

"Look sir," Laura started saying. "I do not want to disappoint you, but, you know what? I must look physically to Nora. I am sure I am. But I am not her. If you made an effort and listened carefully to me, you would realise I do not talk like her."

The mature man began to feel frightened; it was as if Laura was serenely telling him the truth.

"I can proof I am not your daughter," Laura continued saying. "You will be able to realise this, the moment you see the medical records.

The father stood up from the beach chair and started to walk backwards while horror appeared on his face, the horror of disappointment, the horror caused by the terrible cruelty his destiny was giving him.

"You are lying," he mumbled, desperate to continue believing. "You are a sick girl."

"No sir," Laura answered. "I am a very sane girl, and I would like to help you find Nora, your daughter..."

The man looked fixedly into her eyes. The pain was coming out of his eyes.

"Show me your right arm," he said to Laura.

She immediately understood what he meant. She right away lifted the sleeve of the silk blouse Vinci had giving her. The father looked at her arm in detail. A second later he sighed and looked at the floor. He sat in the beach chair again. He put a cigarette in his mouth. His hand trembled a little while he lit it.

"You are not my Nora..." he mumbled disappointed. "My daughter had a birthmark which looked like a butterfly on her left arm... My girl is still missing."

Laura put her arm on the shoulders of the devastated man.

"I had already told you I was not your daughter," she told him. "No, please tell me what this is all about... You said you were sure she was going to go back to the clinic. Does she work there?"

"No," the father answered. "But that man Vinci works there."

Hearing that name was a shock for Laura. She instantly knew that something had invaded her world and that everything would change; the mature man, the confusion of the faces, and even Wallace story about Vinci's dark past. All of this would inevitably change her life.

"What is wrong with Vinci?" her voice seemed to shudder.

"He was Nora's plastic surgeon," the father answered, while he let a mouthful of smoke escape. "Nora Bardin. We are form Garden City, Kansas. My name is John Frank. Please call me like this."

"I will."

"My daughter had an accident three years ago. It seriously disfigured her face. She needed a miracle. She worked as a teacher at one of the public schools which had that plastic from Florida as its benefactor. Vinci also worked in one of the hospitals we have in Kansas. He was supposed to be very famous." John Frank sighed. He shyly continued: "he did an amazing job. He reconstructed Nora's face and changed it completely. She was very beautiful after the surgery... Look, let me show you." He looked for a Photograph of Nora in his wallet. He took it out and showed it to Laura.

Laura looked at it.

"Oh my God!" she said out of breath. "That is..."

"That is you," John Frank whispered.

"Someone who looks incredible like me," Laura admitted. "I do not understand. I did not say this before... Vinci is also my surgeon. I also suffered an accident. My face was also disfigured. My face was also reconstructed and changed. I thought it was an exclusive face. What is this doctor doing?

"That is something I would like to know?" John Frank said.

"Tell me more about Nora..." Laura asked.

"She had already had her surgery," John Frank continued. "But she had to go back to Vinci for backups whenever he came to Kansas. Then one day she said, she had discovered something about that guy. Without Vinci noticing, she had looked at his medical records. I do not remember the details of the way she discovered it, but she said it worried her."

"What did she discover?"

"She did not want to tell me."

"Did you at least have a clue?"

"No. But she continued seeing Vinci. And then one day, she disappeared."

"Disappeared? Just like that?"

"Yes, it happened one afternoon. She left the school where she worked. And nobody saw her again. Her car was found somewhere near the highway. The police have been investigating the case, but they have not found out anything yet."

"And what about Vinci?"

"I have to say he has been acting excellent, actually. He came to visit me as soon as he knew that Nora had gone missing. He always keeps contact with me, although he advised me not to make her disappearance too public."

"Why not?" Laura said surprised.

"He said that if my daughter's photograph and the fact she was missing were made public, this would only cause the attention of psychopaths…"

"Oh, I see," Laura said. "… I am really sorry about everything, Mister Bardin."

John Frank put the photograph of his beloved daughter back in his wallet again, and looked fixedly at Laura one more time. His tired eyes looked at her from top to bottom.

"You look so much like her. He wore her hair the same way. Vinci introduced her to a famous hairdresser from Los Angeles. And she also wore very similar clothes to you."

Laura felt a shiver run down her spine. Was she by any change Nora Bardin's clone? Why had Vinci created two similar faces? Did he duplicate women? And what had happened to Nora?

"This must be very difficult for you," Laura said. She paused for a moment and then she continued: "have you got any clue about what could have happened to you daughter?"

"No," John Frank answered as he let a mouthful of smoke escape from his mouth. "Doctor Vinci said she could probably have run away. He said that women that went through that kind of surgery simply wanted a new life. But Nora was not like that. She was always really close to her family." He hesitated for a moment. "I had no idea where she could be... I have looked for her everywhere. I have not found her. That is the reason I came back here." He stopped talking for a moment. He sighed. "This week is a year of her surgery. I though she would come back to the private clinic, that she maybe would seek contact with Vinci. I came to Florida just because I had hoped to see my daughter near the clinic... All of this is very strange for me."

"I understand," Laura said. "It is also strange for me. I think you daughter and me are involved in something really bizarre. And we are involved because of Francesco Vinci," she reflected for a moment. Then she said disappointed: "something is really wrong in all of this, Mister Bardin... and I will find out what it is it."

"I will help you," John Frank said. "I have the feeling you are... almost Nora. Maybe you could come to Garden City. You can go through my daughter's things. The things she wrote down about her work. You have been in touch with Vinci. Maybe you can come up with something new."

"That is a marvellous idea. I am going to go to Garden City..." Laura stopped talking. "Would you like a cup of coffee?"

"No, no," John Frank answered. "I have spent too much time here already." He coughed. "The only thing I want is to go back to Kansas city, to be home again... I will give you my address and my telephone number." He wrote it down on a piece of paper. "Please come as soon as you can, Miss Duncan."

"I will, do not worry," Laura said. She thought about the situation again. Then she looked at Nora's father and said: "But you know something? There is something that would maybe be convenient for both of us…"

"What?" John Frank asked.

"Do not talk about any of this to Vinci. Do not, get close to him. If Vinci finds out we have met, and if he is trying to hide something, things could get complicated for us. Do you understand what I am trying to say, Mister Bardin?"

The man nodded. He stood up fast. He said good bye to Laura and went out of the porch.

He walked to the corner of the street. He stopped a taxi and disappeared as quickly as he had arrived.

Laura thought that her trip from the clinic, which had been planned as a serene and a quiet journey, had become a nightmare… The great plastic surgeon, who had been her blessed a miraculous hero, was maybe a perverted creature, manipulative, someone with a dark past and able of doing sinister things.

She suddenly thought about Nora Bardin' face. Her own face! Why had that girl form Kansas strangely disappeared?... She could not help to feel a shiver running down her spine, when she thought about the fact that her own life could be in danger.

*   *

5

"Larry, I think Francesco Vinci gave the face of another woman," Laura said to her friend.

Wallace and she were sitting at the kitchen table in Laura's house. They were eating some delicious smoked salmons with asparaguses and some white wine. Sometime after noon, Laura had called Wallace to the Miami Globe offices, and had invited him to have dinner at her house that night. She had told him she some interesting things to tell him. The journalist and her artistic manager accepted the invitation immediately.

"What did you say?" Wallace asked incredulously.

"Listen carefully," Laura continued talking, while she cut some piece of salmon. "When I got out of the clinic this morning an older man followed me. It seemed somebody that was mentally disturbed. He talked to me the minute I had reached my house. He thought I was his daughter. His daughter also had had an accident and Vinci had also reconstructed her face. He showed me a picture of his daughter. She was identical to me, Larry."

"You are hallucinating," Wallace said, while chewed some asparaguses.

"No, absolutely not." Laura replied. Larry, I saw the photograph."

"I think you are taking some sort of medicine that makes you hallucinate."

"I am not taking anything damned! If you had been there, you would not be saying these things. Vinci gave me the face of another woman.

"And where is that other lady?"

"She has disappeared."

"Oh my God!"

"It is strange, isn't it?" Laura said. She started to tell Larry the details about the conversations she had had with john Frank Bardin.

Wallace listened very carefully, without interrupting Laura. When she had finished talking, there was a big silence between them both. The journalist was trying to make sense about what he had just heard.

"Laura," he finally said. "If what you have just told me is true…"

"It is true, Larry," Laura interrupted him. "I think I am able to distinguish the truth from a bunch of crap."

"Then," Wallace continued while he ate: "this means Vinci has committed one of the most horrendous acts in the history of Medicine… Besides the fact that that man is a fraud… and he is mentally ill."

Laura nodded. She poured two glasses of wine.

"This sounds like the plot of a terror movie," Larry joked around. He finished his plate of salmon and asparaguses and started to drink some wine. "The satanic Doctor Vinci and his faces…"

Laura did not smile. Larry's joke did not seem funny to her. She also finished her dinner and drank some white wine. The wine tasted a bit too cold she thought to herself. Wallace finished his wine and impulsively grabbed the bottle, poured himself another glass and drank it. Laura remembered that Larry had told her his father, who was the parish priest, had suddenly died because of alcohol intoxication after drinking several bottles of champagne in a party. Laura imagined her friend in the same situation and the comparison depressed her.

At that moment the phone rang in the kitchen. Laura answered it, expecting to find the voice of some other friend welcoming her back home on the other side of the line. But she was wrong…

"Miss Duncan?"

Laura felt a shudder in her stomach. She knew that fine and arrogant voice perfectly well.

"Miss Duncan, this is doctor Vinci speaking."

It was the man she was started to mistrust.

"Doctor…" she mumbled. She stopped talking for a moment. Then she lied: "How nice to hear your voice!"

"Well Miss Duncan, first of all, I want to apologise for not being present this morning when you left the clinic."

"Do not worry about that," she said. Larry turned around and looked strangely at her.

"I was just calling to see how you were doing," Vinci continued saying.

"Oh I am doing just fine. I am really doing fine."

"Do you have some kind of pain in your hands or in you face?"

"Yes, but just a little," Laura admitted.

"I have told you that is quite normal; it is caused by the tightness of the implants," Vinci replied. "You will not feel a thing in a few months. The first few weeks after the surgery are always the most difficult ones. Be careful with the cool wind and cold water."

"I will, doctor."

"And you can come round my office in the clinic whenever you want."

"Yes doctor."

Just a minute later the great plastic surgeon hung up. Laura thought about everything she had just found out about the doctor. Maybe his geniality was tricky, because her face was not exclusively hers. It was the good copy of another face. Vinci copied faces… And the woman to whom the original face belonged had disappeared in mysterious circumstances.

Larry poured his third glass of wine and asked her:

"Was it that guy?"

"Yes," Laura answered. "HE wanted to know how I was doing." She left the kitchen. She opened a window in the hallway and went out in to the back yard of the house. It was a warm, starry and calm night. Laura listened to the birds sing. She laid in the hammock and lit a cigarette. She had not smoked for weeks. Why did she now? Maybe she felt nervous about something.

Just a little while later, Larry came out into the back yard with another glass of wine in his hand.

"This expensive shit is very good," Wallace said referring to the wine.

Laura did not say anything. She just looked at the Mozart and Debussy scores laying on the table in the back yard. She would have some time for them in the future, she thought. For the time being, she had something she had to do... something that was unavoidable. She finished her cigarette, looked at Wallace and said:

"I am going to Kansas tomorrow, Larry. I am going to Nora Bardin's house."

"What are you saying...?"

"I have to investigate this matter in-depth. I want to talk to that girl's father again. I want to know what is behind her disappearance.

"Honey, suddenly you have become an investigator."

"I suppose I have a very good nose for things like this," Laura answered. "Remember that my father was a police officer. I have probably inherited this instinct from him."

Larry let his heavily built body fall down next to Laura on the hammock.

"I think you are right, honey," Wallace said. "If I were you, I would also fell incredibly curious to know what happened. Will you go alone to Kansas?"

"Do you want to come with me?"

"I am sorry, but I can not even if I wanted," Wallace answered. "I am too busy at the newspaper."

"Well, I do not care, I will go alone then," Laura said. "I am big enough to take care of my own."

"Be careful anyway," Larry said. They kissed.

*   *

At the same moment Laura fiercely decided to get involved in a business that could have consequences beyond any suspicion, Doctor Francesco Vinci was heading towards the television studio next to his office, once again. He prepared the video to record himself again. As usual, nobody else would be present, and afterwards the recording would be kept in a safe, whose combination only he knew.

All of his recordings were precious to Vinci, although this one was decisive. He had already recorded some videos in which he talked about the work he had performed on Nora Bardin. The same Nora Bardin whose father had already contacted Laura. Now, Vinci would make the last video about Nora, completing the package of video tapes he had started when she had first entered his office in the hospital in Kansas City.

He immediately turned the lights on in the studio. He combed his abundant dark hair, and he straightened his tie with a diamante in the middle. He turned the camera on and looked directly into it.

"Ladies and gentlemen," he started saying. Tonight is a sad night for me, because I do not like to admit I made a mistake. But I have to do it. Science is full of mistakes... During the last two sessions, I have been talking about the work I performed on Nora Bardin, from Kansas. You will remember that the trouble started when the skin did not straighten the way I had projected it would and some of the muscles became tense unexpectedly." He stopped talking for a moment. "It became obvious I could not present her face to world as the most perfect face, as the greatest achievement in the art of plastic surgery, as the face of the twenty first century...

The experiment had failed... But I decided to duplicate essential element of that face. However there were some inconveniences to this. What could I do about Nora? Would

there be two women with the same face walking around?"
He stopped talking for a little longer now than before…
"Ladies and gentlemen, we all know that one has to make sacrifices in the name of science. We see this everyday in Medicine. New drugs and surgical techniques that produce a high rate of mortality before they are improved… It was obvious to me that the perfect face I had proposed to create should be exclusive. It should not be similar to any other one. That is why I made the difficult, but necessary, decision to eliminate Nora Bardin to be able to duplicate and improve her face on some other woman…" He stopped talking once more. He cleared his throat and took some breath. Then he continued: "still I did not want to loose her completely as an individual for my investigation. A surgeon can always learn; even from his own imperfections…"

At that moment, Francesco Vinci stood up from his chair and walked towards a closet that was hermetically closed. He opened it and took out something that was wrapped in a white piece of cloth. He put it on the table. Then, the hands of the great surgeon, softly unwrapped the thing on the table… A jar appeared which had some green liquid inside it; and also the head of a woman.

"Ladies and gentlemen, I introduce you to Nora Bardin," Vinci said. "But I will not give up; I will continue working to achieve the goal I have put for myself."

*   *

6

It was already becoming evening in the wheat fields of Kansas.

After driving round one of the wheat fields, the bus stopped, in the middle of a cloud of dust, in front of the Post Office of Garden City. The door of the bus opened and the first person to get of was Laura, holding a lizard skinned bag.

Then she walked toward the taxi stand. She found one and gave the driver an address.

"I know that street, madam," the taxi driver answered. "I can take you there."

Laura nodded. She opened the back door of the taxi and got in. She leaned the back of the seat a little.

The driver smiled through the rear-view mirror, thinking that the attractive face of that stranger looked familiar to him.

The taxi drove away. Then, after riding for a few blocks, a police car discreetly appeared behind the taxi. Inside the taxi, Laura carefully turned her head a little; just enough to see the two police officers through the window of the taxi. It were two quite fat men and they did not look very friendly. One of them had an enormous head that looked like an elephant head. He made a gesture to his partner on the wheel of the police car.

Suddenly the police man behind the wheel of the police car accelerated and put the car next to the taxi. The elephant head shouted at the taxi driver:

"Could you please stop the taxi, Joe?"

"What is the matter guys?" the taxi driver asked the police officers.

"Just do as you are told, Joe," elephant head insisted.

The taxi driver shrugged his shoulders and looked at Laura through rear-view mirror.

"I have to stop, madam..." he apologised. "I do not know what is going on..."

Laura knitted her brow. The only thing she wanted was to get to the Bardin's house as soon as possible. She did not say anything, but she was annoyed.

The taxi stopped at one side of the street and the taxi driver stayed behind the wheel while the two police officers got out of the police car and walked towards the taxi. But they did not talk to the taxis driver, they talked to Laura.

"Madam," elephant head said. "Could we have a word with you?"

Immediately, Laura sensed something strange had happened. But, what?

"What...what is the matter?" she hesitated.

"I think you what is matter," the ironic voice of the other police officer answered.

"No, I do not know..."

"Are you Nora Bardin?"

Laura felt her heart beat very fast. She had the impression she would suffer one of those anxiety attacks she had had when she was a child. These attacks happened whenever she was under great stress. They had not happened to her for years and she thought she had overcome them. Maybe she had not.

"No I am not," she answered. You must confuse me for somebody else. I..."

"Will you please accompany us, madam?" Elephant Head continued saying, while he opened the back door of the taxi. He told the taxi driver: "Do not worry, Joe; this is only a domestic problem."

"No, you are making a mistake," Laura replied vehemently, and trying to avoid those thick police hands to grab her. "You should simply call her father, Mister Bardin. I talked to him a few days ago... I really look like Nora, that is all... but I am not her... I am visiting Mister Bardin..."

"Please, just come with us, madam," Elephant Head insisted. "Please do not make it harder than it should be. You are a reported missing person."

"No, I am not."

"We are here to help you," the other police officer said. Immediately after that, he and elephant head grabbed Laura's arms and dragged her out of the taxi. She resisted vigorously, repeating time and time again she was not Nora Bardin... But they would not listen to her. The police officers surely thought she was mentally ill, that she did not know who she was.

"Are you going to arrest me?" she muttered. "I am a pianist from Miami."

"Well, you can play the piano at the police station..."

Laura tried to reach for her ID card in her purse, but the two police man held her arms to her back and pushed her towards the police car.

"Stop it!" Laura yelled desperately. "You are making a mistake. I look like Nora that is all. But I am not her, damned!"

They did not talk to her again. They simply forced her inside the police car and drove away fast, as some people on the streets looked at them as they had just arrested a criminal.

Laura was sitting in the backseat together with Elephant Head.

"If only you would listen to me," Laura protested knowing it was useless. "I have my ID card."

They did not even look at her.

"We will take you to the police station, everything will be all right," Elephant Head said after a while. "If you give us more trouble, we will call a doctor."

"I do not need a doctor," Laura said. "I am not crazy."

"But you are behaving like you are," the other police officer ironically answered behind the wheel.

The police car drove away with screeching tyres.

*   *

"Please, take a seat, madam," the grey haired police officer said. "I am Sergeant Hendricks, and I just want to ask you some questions.

"Laura sat on a hard chair. She was a bit more calm that before. Her curious eyes looked carefully around the police station which had thick cream coloured painted walls and filing cabinets. The place smelled like coffee. She thought that was kind of strange, but then again, she had never been in a police station before in her life. Never. Even though her father, according to what her mother had told her, had been a police officer. In one way or the other, she was suspicious of that kind of places. Maybe it made her think of her bastard father, the same person who had left her before she had even been born.

She realized the Sergeant was giving orders to the two police officers who had taken her there. He managed to hear one of them say she was a mentally disturbed lady.

A moment later, Laura heard some footsteps behind her. She turned around. She saw somebody walk toward her in the hall way of the police station…John Frank Bardin. The man was wearing the same woollen jacket Laura already knew. And he had a cigarette hanging in his mouth.

Laura stood up.

They stood face to face to each other. None of them said a word, until a smile appeared on John Frank's face. It was an embarrassed smile, just as if he was the responsible of the trouble Laura was in at that moment.

"Well, madam," elephant said to Laura. "Are you not going to kiss your father?"

"No…" Laura Duncan, who was the exact copy of a sweet girl from Garden City named Nora Bardin, answered.

*   *

7

John Frank's house was located on Mayor Street. It was a simple building made out of wood with five bedrooms and part of a row of terraced houses. The house looked very clean. Her father had kept it like that, because he wanted his daughter to come back to decent place, when she eventually did come back... some day. Laura doubted she ever would.

On the table was a coloured photograph of Nora taken after the surgery. The photograph instantly froze Laura's blood. She was looking at herself; the face, the features, the hairstyle, the Italian designer's clothes... Everything the great plastic surgeon Francesco Vinci had suggested to change about her physical appearance... what was that man planning for Nora? And why did Nora, with that beautiful new face, disappear so suddenly?

"Would you like something to drink, Miss Duncan? John Frank asked her while both of them sat in the living room. "You must be hungry too, after the trip all the way from Florida, and after the experience with the town police officers."

"Yes, I am," Laura admitted. "Anything you have will be fine."

Mister Bardin went to the kitchen. Laura could hear the sound of crystal glasses being fetched. She leaned back on the sofa; she relaxed her arms and crossed her legs. She sighed, and suddenly had the feeling she was an outsider, invading that house, worrying that poor father even more, while the only thing he wanted to see his darling daughter again.

John Frank returned to the living room with two glasses of cognac. He gave one of them to Laura and kept one for himself.

"Do you know something?" Mister Bardin started telling her. "That Mister Vinci called me shortly after the meeting we had... And I did what you asked me to do. I did not mention we had met. The guy called to say he wanted to maintain contact with me... And to calm me down..."

"Calm you down?"

"As I had already told you before in Miami, Vinci thinks that some women that undergo such a plastic surgery want to change their entire life afterwards and that they leave... but they almost always come back."

"Laura did not answer, but she thought she would not believe in everything that Vinci told her. She sipped a bit of cognac while she remembered the reason behind her trip there. She said to mister Bardin:

"You mentioned Nora had found out something about Vinci when she had read his file in his office. You also said you did not know what that something was."

"No, she never told me."

"It must have been something bad..."

"Yes; that is also what I think," John frank said. "But; what?" she shrugged his shoulders and sipped some more cognac.

"Do the police have some theory?

"They are not really interested in the case. They have handled it, as the typical missing person case. Nothing really important."

"I would like to see the things Nora left behind, if you do not mind," Laura said.

"Of course I do not. I have organised the best I could," John Frank explained, while he finished his cognac. "I went through them one more time. I think you will not find anything."

"Let me try."

"Please follow me, Miss Duncan."

The bedroom that belonged to that identical image of her was simple. It was painted pink and it had yellow curtains. There was a single bed, decorated with the images of fishes and little animals which were obviously part of Nora's childhood. On the wall, there were some posters of popular films, some calendars and a collection of dolls on a shelf. There also was a cupboard and a chest of drawers.

"The room is exactly like it was when my daughter was last in it," John Frank said. "I just cleaned and tidied it a little. You can go through the chest of drawers if you want to. You will find a folder with some of her things in the top drawer. There are some notes, holiday letters, her photo album and some telephone messages. Her address book is on the night table."

"I will be careful with all of that," Laura said.

"I know you will," John Frank smiled. "I will leave you alone now."

Laura nodded. Mister Bardin disappeared slowly, just like he had in Florida. But this time, he had gone into his own bedroom to wait. Laura sensed that that poor man did not really believe she would find anything in that room, which would help to get some clue about his daughter's mysterious disappearance. The police had searched more than once and had come up with nothing. Well, up to that moment there had only been disappointment in everything that was related to the disappearance of that small town and beautiful young woman. Nevertheless, John Frank still hoped to find her. Laura thought that john Frank's love towards Nora must be unconditional. She felt a bit jealous of Nora for that. She wished she had had such an affectionate and responsible father as Mister Bardin.

Laura had a strange feeling when she started to search the room. In that bedroom, a duplicated face, Vinci's other masterpiece, had slept and breathed... Her twin had maybe left forever, and would not come back...

She started to look through the chest of drawers. She found some elegant and exclusively designed clothes, which probably had been presents bought by the generous surgeon. But none of that was of any use to find an answer to Nora disappearance.

Then she looked through the folder. She read a letter that Nora had sent home on a holiday trip to Denver and some postcards she had sent from a summer holiday resort in New Mexico when she had been recovering after the plastic surgery. That did not indicate any clue about he disappearance either. In none of the letters or postcards she mentioned Francesco Vinci.

While she was going through some more pieces of papers and telephone messages, Laura started to come to same conclusion that Mister Bardin and the police had come; there was nothing there.

She started to go through Nora's little address book, she slowly turned every page, read every name, address, telephone numbers, new telephone numbers. Every number had a name and a last name corresponding to it and an address... Everything looked normal. There was not anything suspicious there either. Laura turned another page... Nothing.

Laura put the address book back on the night table. She lay on the bed and closed her eyes thinking about another place in that bedroom where there could be a clue that would help her find the answers she needed... Then she remembered, she had not gone through the cupboard yet.

She rose from the bed. The elegant clothes hung from plastic clothes hangers in the cupboard. Laura's curious hand went through Nora's elegant clothes, thinking that everybody forgets something in the pockets. But she found nothing... A second later, she was feeling inside the inner pocket of a suede jacket and suddenly her fingers found a piece of paper. It was the ticket to some night club show in the city of Las Vegas, Nevada... What was that ticket doing in that pocket? Had Nora been in that night club? Why?

Somebody knocked on the door of the bedroom. It was John Frank. He was holding the bottle of cognac in his hand and he seemed a little drunk. He looked at Laura a bit annoyed and dryly asked:

"Did you already finish going through my daughters things...?"

"Yes," Laura answered. She looked at her watch. She had been going through things in that room for almost two hours. She sighed and looked at the ticket in her hand. "Did Nora go to Las Vegas, Mister Bardin?"

The old man drank from the bottle without any hurry and answered:

"No that I know of... Why do you ask?"

"I found a ticket to a nightclub in that city."

"A nightclub?" John Frank wrinkled his forehead. "What would my daughter want in a place like that?" He walked towards Laura. "Please, let me see the ticket."

Laura gave it to him. John Frank took the ticket and looked at it carefully.

"I have no idea what this is, Miss Duncan," he said after a while. "Nora never mentioned she had travelled to Las Vegas... Where did you find this?"

"I found it in one of the inner pockets of the suede jacket in the cupboard."

Mister Bardin winked but did not say anything. He yawned. Suddenly he seemed very tired. Tired and drunk. Laura pointed at the ticket John Frank was still holding in his hand and asked him:

"Can I keep that?"

"Sure," the old man said and gave the ticket to Laura.

She took it and told herself that if Nora's father did not know anything about a trip to Las Vegas, than neither did the police. Laura sighed and felt certain she had found something interesting related to Nora's disappearance. She was convinced that Nora Bardin had travelled to Las Vegas and had not mentioned it to her dad because of some powerful reason.

She looked at the ticket again. The nightclub was called Old Sand and it was located on Paradise Road. She kept the ticket in her bag. And then she had a memory flash... Something Larry Wallace had mentioned about Doctor Vinci. *The guy likes to have fun once in a while, and squander lots of money. Sometimes he goes to Las Vegas where he flirts*

*with dancers and plays a lot of money on roulette games in
the casinos.'*

Vinci had also gone to Las Vegas…

Laura warmly said good bye to Mister Bardin. She left the
house and also Garden City.

* *

8

No problem whatsoever happened on Laura's trip back
to the humidity of Miami. The first thing she did when she
arrived home in South beach was to call the newspaper where
Larry Wallace worked.

That evening, Larry went to her house, where they ate
Chinese food bought by the journalist and they talked.
Wallace loved Oriental food, just as much as Laura's
chardonnay wine.

"Maybe the answer is in Las Vegas," Laura started to
say to her friend. "Nora Bardin was there, in that night club,
the old sand, and I do not think she went there on holidays or
whatever. But why did she not tell her father about that trip?
She probably found out something strange in Las Vegas…
We both know Vinci used to have fun in Nevada."

"What is your point in all of this?" Wallace asked, as
he tasted the rice with some sauce and some pieces of fish.

"My intuition is telling me that Nora's
disappearance is directly related to something she must have
found in that nightclub. Something that linked her and Vinci
and maybe a third person…"

"Explain yourself a little better, please," Wallace asked.

""Larry," Laura sighed. "I have been thinking about this since I left Kansas with this ticket in my hands... It is a nightclub in Las Vegas. What can you find in those places? Well, beautiful women; dancers, waitresses..." she stopped talking for a minute. "Do you know something? I think that if Vinci made such similar face in to very distant places geographically; Miami and Garden City; It is very possible he might have done the same in Las Vegas."

Wallace was reluctant."Three identical faces? I think you are making your own hypothesis up."

"I do not think so," Laura said vigorously. "Stop and think for a moment. Everything makes sense, Larry. What did Nora Bardin find out about Vinci from his medical record that could have disturbed her? She could have discovered the same thing I discovered when I saw Nora's father standing in front of my door: Francesco Vinci is creating an assembly line using one face as the model."

"It is possible," Wallace mumbled. He finished his Chinese food and drank some white wine from his glass. Laura had also finished her plate. She did not like Chinese food very much. But she sacrificed her palate now, to please Larry. She put her plate to one side, and served to cups of tea with cinnamon. She gave one of the cups to Larry, who was already drinking his third glass of wine.

"Stop drinking wine, Take this instead," Laura said while she showed him the cup of tea.

Wallace wrinkled his forehead for a while.

"Alright," he answered then. He fooled around with his cup, before he drank the tea in one big gulp. He put both his elbows on the table and said: "do you want to know something honey? You I do not like that arrogant Vinci guy. He is to full of himself. But I also do not want to lynch him. Laura, the things we are talking about are dynamite, but we do not have any real proof. He did this with two faces... Ok, it was something perverse. However, everything else is just a theory."

"You are right," Laura mumbled. "I am letting myself go to fast because of a hunch. But it is a good hunch."

Wallace put a cigarette between his teeth. "When will you see Vinci again?" he asked.

"Tomorrow," Laura answered. "A routine check up."

"Try not to say too much," Wallace advised her. He lit the cigarette.

Laura nodded. She sipped the last bit of tea she had and stood up from the table. She walked out of the kitchen.

"Larry, let's go to the living room," she told her friend. "I want to practice Chopin a little."

"Yes, honey," Wallace smiled. "I have always liked watching you play piano."

*   *

While Larry and Laura were having dinner in Laura's house; somewhere else in that same area of the South of Florida, in an elegant mansion in Palm Beach, Doctor Vinci was lying on bed in his bedroom and was caressing the breasts of an attractive nurse who worked at his clinic and had accepted to spend the night with him. Although Vinci's sexual life was a bit more complex than the average human being, at that moment Vinci was not thinking about having sex or about that female lying besides him. His mind, his twisted mind was focused on the experiment he had been obsessed about for years... He had a little doubt about something. There were always doubts in medical investigation... What would happen if his experiment with Laura Duncan did not go as he was expecting? If that beautiful face did not heal correctly he would have no to her choice but to get rid of her. He would not have any trouble in inventing some story to back it up. After that he would continue trying, new women, new attempts, until he reached success.

He thought about the pathetic image of Nora Bardin. What a shame! But everything was justified. At least that was what he always repeated in his mind.

Everything was perfectly justified.

Until then, everything with Laura seemed to go without any problems. The next step would be to talk with that woman and tell her about the plans he had for her. He had to convince to give her career as a pianist up, and make her fortune out of her face. He would have her try a career in the modelling and cosmetics world. Who would not be attracted by the wealth and fame that could come from all of that?

And she owed him… He gave birth to her again.

In some way, Francesco Vinci had safe her from her terrible fate. Her career and her life were almost over after that horrible fire that burnt her face. But he reconstructed it for her, making it even more beautiful and fabulous.

After a little while he thought about another face… But this time it was not perfect… Scylla Dubois, from New Orleans… A new mistake… A new and fucking mistake!... A stain on his reputation.

He would have to do something about Scylla… Everything was justified in the world of doctor Vinci.

* *

9

Many miles away from Miami, in the state of Texas, a black car from belong to the investigation police of the city of Dallas stopped near a cliff full of bushes. Lieutenant Jack Petersen and one of his officers got out of the car together with another man; old, wearing a beard as well as worn out clothes and who stank of crap.

The lieutenant and the other detective each lit their flashlights. Petersen ask the man who lived on the street:

"Where is the body, Slim?"

"A bit more down that way," the old man mumbled. He pointed to the bottom of the cliff. "I will show you the way. Follow me."

The detectives nodded.

The old man started to walk down the hill in silence. The way was narrow and surrounded by bushes. Both detectives followed him, thinking they would find yet another corpse abandoned there among the bushes.

Two minutes later the man stopped. He sighed and nervously wiped his bearded face. He reluctantly pointed at one side of the way.

The detectives tried to see something with their flashlights. First their saw the legs, then the torso and the arms… they could not find the head, but it was the corpse of a woman.

It was a repulsive scenario. But both detectives were used to these kinds of findings. It surely was the work of some disturbed criminal.

Behind the detectives, the man threw up.

*   *

The psychiatrist recommended by Vinci for Laura's post surgical therapy was called Alan Jung. He was around fifty five years old and he was single. He divided his time between his patients and his classes at the university. According to what Laura had heard, he was a specialist in personality disorders.

The psychiatrist's office was located in a ancient mansion, which had roman columns and gardens on Biscayne Boulevard. It had no secretary and the place was warm and friendly.

"Come in Miss Duncan," the doctor said to Laura. "Doctor Vinci has already told me about your miraculous recovery and some of the other details of your case. But I never imagined you were so attractive…"

Jung's voice was soft, flattering and fatherly. Laura was sure that everybody must like that voice. It invited you to tell your problems.

After the initial introductions, Jung asked Laura to lie down on his comfortable couch.

"Now," the psychiatrist said as he sat down at spinning chair in front of Laura. "Let's start by talk about you, Miss Duncan. I want to hear everything about you."

Laura's voice sounded a bit hesitating and reluctant at the beginning. She was rather a reserved person and she had never felt comfortable ventilating her personal problems before others. However, she slowly relaxed and became confident. She saw Doctor Jung as a confidant, not so as a doctor. She talked about her lonely and difficult childhood. Her father's abandonment at birth. The loss of her only sister and of her mother. Her university studies in music, thanks to the support of a priest, who had seen her once playing distractedly on the organ of the church, and had sensed her enormous musical potential.

Alan Jung listened very carefully and interested to Laura. This professional seemed to have infinite patience and comprehension for other people's problems.

After a while, Jung himself started to orient Laura with routine questions he always used to ask to anyone that had had an important plastic surgery.

"Do you feel uncomfortable if people look at you now?"

"No not really, no," Laura answered. "I noticed they do, but it is flattering. I suppose it is vanity."

"I guess it is," Jung admitted. "We are vain one way or the other. Women especially, if you do not mind me saying so." He stopped talking for a moment. And what about your closest friends and relatives? They must notice the difference?"

"Sure, but this was not a cosmetic surgery. It was because of an accident. I do not think they think of it the same way."

"All right. Are you suffering some kind of identity confusing? Do you look in the mirror and wonder who you are?"

"Sometimes," Laura answered. "I mean, this face is extremely beautiful, but it is not mine. It feels like I were a stranger... Sometimes I feel like that, although I will have to get accustomed to this new faced."

"You will get accustomed to it, Miss Duncan. You should not worry about that." The psychiatrist stopped talking again. Then he asked: "do you feel guilty about your surgery?"

"Feel guilty?"

"It happens to everyone," Jung said. "It is something really common of the conscious of humans. For example, when a friend of ours has a serious accident at work and is seriously disabled, everybody feels a bit guilty to be healthy... In your case, your face has been reconstructed by a great surgeon... And still I am sure you know a lot of people that have suffered similar accidents, and have to live in the shadows for the rest of their lives."

I suppose I was very lucky," Laura admitted. "I thank God for it."

Doctor Jung tilted his head and said:

"It is not every day that a patient is as lucky to have such a notable specialist as Francesco Vinci to reconstruct their destroyed face."

Once again the distinctive image and almost miraculous of the great plastic surgeon appeared thought Laura. Then she felt a bit confused, and wondered if Jung knew about Vinci's turbulent past. Did he know something about the strange case of the duplication of faces she had just discovered?... He probably did not.

Laura's entire body became tense on the couch. She had brief idea. She doubted... But, as she felt very curious, she decided to venture a little, even knowing she was sailing in dangerous waters. She understood that Vinci had committed medical negligence; and he had to be punished for it. She plucked up courage and told the understanding doctor Jung:

"Can... Can I ask you a question?"

The psychiatrist nodded.

"I wish to be entirely honest with you, doctor..."

"Go ahead. What is it about?"

Laura made a long pause. She sighed. *'How do I tell him? How can I tell him what I discovered about the man that gave m back my life? Maybe I am going to ruin his reputation... But the two identical faces seem to make me think differently...'*

"Go ahead, Miss Duncan," Jung insisted. "You have to trust me completely. I will always be there for you. Form the moment you came into the door of my office this morning, you are my patient, part of my thoughts and you have all my attention." He moved his chair a bit closer to Laura. "Is it something delicate?"

"A little?" Laura pressed her lips together before she started to talk. "It is about doctor Vinci. He is a great surgeon, but..." She stopped and sighed again. "But I have discovered that... I have discovered..." She hesitated. She asked Jung:

"could I smoke her in the office? I mean, would you mind if I did?"

"Please do if you want to," the doctor said.

Laura lit a cigarette.

"Do you know something?" she continued releasing the smoke softly from her mouth. "I have discovered that Vinci gave the exact same face he gave to me...exactly the same... to another patient... In Kansas."

There was a thick and cold silence between Laura and the doctor. Jung nervously winked. Laura felt her knees tremble.

"I do not really understand you," Jung said then. "Could you please be more explicit?"

Then Laura told him about her meeting with Mister John Frank Bardin and the conversation they had.

"I see," Jung said when Laura had finished telling him about the situation. "I have never heard anything like this before..." he closed his eyes for a moment. "You said that that girl named Nora had disappeared?"

"Yes, she simply disappeared. She disappeared from the face of the earth. But the incident I had with the police in Kansas and the photograph I saw show the amazing similarity of our faces. And we were seen by the same doctor. By Vinci..."

Jung thought for a moment.

"So, you are upset," he slowly said, "because another woman looks like you. Is that the problem?"

"No." Laura shook her head. "It seems you still do not understand. What upsets me is that Doctor Vinci gave the same face to two women. I do not think that is correct, not ethical. What do you think?"

"Of course it is not ethical," Jung answered.

"And what also bother me, is the fact that she has strangely disappeared. According to her father, Nora, was a family person. And besides that I have other suspicions."

"Like what?"

"I think that Vinci has probably given this face to more women."

The psychiatrist winked nervously again.

"Do you any proof of what you are saying?"

"I do not want to talk about that yet," Laura said, gasping exhaling the smoke of her cigarette. "I am still following some clues."

Jung stroke his jaw with his hand. He took his glasses off. He sank deep into his own reflections. Then he muttered:

"Damned, this is very serious. Look, it is very difficult for me to decide if what you are saying is true." He cleaned his glasses with his tie. He put them on and continued saying: "do you something? Even the greatest doctors do thing that would not make them proud. Doctor Vinci could have his reasons to do what you are saying he did."

"Maybe he has," Laura replied. "But his reasons can not be ethical. What he did can not be something that the field of Medicine accepts. No doctor has the right to duplicate faces."

Jung reflected again.

"If we imagine the worst," he said, "that Vinci maybe has duplicated faces to prove he could do it. Do you really fell affected emotionally by it? I mean you have not been directly harmed by it. You are happy with the results of the surgery. Your life has changed."

"That is true," Laura stated. "But what is happening worries me."

"And you want to continue investing this? Maybe you are a bit obsessed by it. For the moment being, you do not have enough evidence to press any charges against Doctor Vinci.

Laura put her cigarette out in the ashtray on the table near the couch.

"I want to find out why he did it," she answered.

Jung's pale face showed signs if disappointment.

"Do whatever you think is best, Miss Duncan." He looked at his golden watch and stood up. He kindly said: "I am very sorry, but our time is up. I have to go to Tampa and visit a patient…"

"Do not worry," Laura said while she stood up from the couch. "I know your time is valuable."

"Miss Duncan, can I ask you something?"

"What?"

"Could you please stay in touch with me? I will guarantee you maximum confidentiality in everything you tell me."

Laura looked at him, and wondered if she could trust that doctor who was an acquaintance of Vinci. She was not very sure about that. However, Alan Jung was also the psychiatrist of the city. A well known professional that maybe would never do something unethical.

"I will, doctor," She finally answered.

Laura left his office. Jung remained standing in the middle of his place of work, listening to Laura's footsteps on the other side of the door.

He thought for a moment. Then he walked towards the window of the office, looking outside to the view he saw everyday. Biscayne Boulevard shone under the burning midday sun. Further down the street was the beach, the sand and the blue sea. He thought that life had been generous to him until that moment. He had prestige and money. Three years ago, he had changed the cold weather from the North East of the country for the warmth of Florida. If everything went as planned, he would retire in that same pleasant place.

But now a problem had come up…

'Confidentiality?' he wondered. 'To hell with confidentiality if one had to save one's skin.'

He grabbed the phone and dialled a number. On the other side of the line a soft and arrogant voice answered.

"Francesco? This is Alan Jung. I think we need to talk."

*   *

10

Doctor Vinci was sitting at his desk analyzing his drawings related to his next intervention; it was a cosmetic facial surgery for the fifty-year-old wife of a computing magnate.

The door of his office suddenly opened. Jung stormed in and sat on one of the chairs. Vinci continued looking at his drawings. He was totally concentrated on his next surgery imagining the big amount of money he would earn from that vain and millionaire woman from California. He stopped looking at his drawings and slowly raised his head. He looked at the psychiatrist.

"What is going on, my friend?" Vinci enquired. "You look a bit pale."

"I do not feel very well," Jung answered.

"What is what you wanted to tell me, Alan?"

Jung swallowed some saliva. He hesitated for a minute and then he said:

"Francesco, this morning I saw one of your patients, Laura Duncan…"

"Oh, yes. I sent her over to you. She is a charming lady. I will also see her this afternoon. A routine check up."

Jung stroke his chin again with one of his hands.

"Something came up during the interview, Francesco." He stopped talking for a moment. "… I do not really know how to tell you… But, have you given her face to somebody else?"

Vinci looked at him attentively.

"What the hell are you talking about, pal?" he asked rudely in a way he had learned in the neighbourhoods of New York. That way of talking was only used by some of his most intimate friends.

"Laura Duncan found someone in Kansas. One of your previous patients, Francesco... The girl assures that when she left the clinic, an older man approached her on her way home and though she was his daughter. The faces were identical, and you had also worked on his daughter's face. His daughter has disappeared."

Vinci could not believe what he was hearing. His heart started beating extremely fast, but he tried not to be obvious. He had to control his emotions. *'That was the key to all of this,'* he said to himself. On the same harsh streets he had learned to hide his fear and panic during his childhood. That way he did not gave the enemy any advantage... But, how did that fool of Bardin know about the new face of Laura so soon? And now, John Frank could start to cause trouble. Maybe he should have killed that old stupid man, together with his daughter... Shit! There had always been a possibility that that high risk experiment could be exposed. But he never thought it would be so sudden. His stomach felt irritated.

"God!" Jung continued saying, while he squeezed his fist together. "You did it again, didn't you, Francesco? You duplicated a face once more. You promised you would not do that again!"

Vinci felt extremely angry. He was not very tolerant when somebody blamed him about something, especially when it involved his job.

"Alright, ok," he confessed. "I admit I did it again. Everything is part of the experiment I mentioned to you a while ago. It is a really revolutionary experience that will change plastic surgery. It is all about trying to reach perfection. To transcend in time. Sometimes one has to take risks in order to reach ones goals... But do not worry, my friend. Everything is still under control."

"I am not very sure about that," Jung replied worried. "The problem is that that girl is going to continue o sniff around. She told me she wanted to find out why you did all of this."

"Damned."

"That changes things, doesn't it? Maybe Laura Duncan is going to become an obstacle. Perhaps she will discover everything and will go to the Police." He grabbed his head. "The most pathetic thing of all this business is that I was your accomplice. I knew you were doing these activities.

"Calm down," Vinci said. "Let me think for a while." Heb stood up from behind his desk and went towards a cupboard. He opened it. He took a bottle of bourbon from inside it. He served two glasses. He gave one of the glasses to Jung and drank from the other one. He meditated about the situation in silence. He finally asked his friend:

"Will you continue being Laura's psychiatrist?"

"Yes." Jung nervously drank his bourbon.

"I need you to get more information from her," Vinci suggested. "And I need to be informed of everything she finds out."

"That is exactly what I intend to do," Jung said. "After all, if you fall, I also fall." He finished his bourbon. He asked for more bourbon to Vinci; He said with a tone of disillusionment: "Do you know something? I sometimes feel like shit as a professional... I promised that girl total confidentiality about everything she would tell me..."

Vinci served Jung another glass and at the same time felt a wave of rage inside his stomach. He fixed his eyes on the psychiatrist and told himself that Jung was weak, a person with absolutely no willpower. He would never accomplish big things... Because of weak professionals like him science and medicine have developed so slowly. Vinci was convinced that to make any progress in the field of science, people had to be audacious and bold. He told his friend:

"The important thing is to stay calm, my friend. Everything has a solution."

The psychiatrist finished his drink with shaky hands. He put the glass on op of the desk, shook his head and asked the surgeon:

"What happened to the other girl?"

"Are talking about Nora?"

"You know very well I am, do not try to pretend to fool me," Jung replied.

"That young woman for Kansas is missing. What do you know about that?

"I have no idea about her," Vinci answered while he tasted the liquor. I suppose that girl was mentally disturbed about her new face. As you already know, not everyone can emotionally handle great beauty that will change their lives.

The intercom of the office sounded twice. The secretary informed the surgeon that someone wanted to talk to him urgently. Vince made a pause and said to Jung:

"Is there anything else you want to tell me?"

The psychiatrist shook his head and sighed. He seemed calmer. Then he stood up from the chair.

"No... I was just about to leave, my friend."

"Remember to keep up to date about our little business."

"Do not worry, Francesco, I will."

When Jung left the office, Vinci answered his telephone conversation.

"Hello?" the surgeon said, thinking it was one of his famous clients.

"Good afternoon, doc," a vulgarly feminine voice mumbled obviously drunk.

Vinci immediately knew who that voice belonged to. He became very angrey and breathed heavily.

"Scylla? But why...? You know you should not call me at my office... You know that."

"Are you afraid that a poor and unimportant person like me mixes too much with your exclusives millionaire clients? Does that bother you?"

"That is not the point, Scylla," Vinci softly said and faked to be calm. "What do you want?"

"I need more money, doc."

"But I sent your cheque less than a week ago."

"I have had some extra expenses, doc."

Shit! Scylla was asking for more money than they had agreed on, Vinci thought to himself. He should never have chosen such a spendthrift as Scylla, to receive a free plastic surgery. He should never have chosen a person that had been in jail... How much longer would Scylla ask him for money? Finally he said:

"I will go to New Orleans in a few days. I will give you some more then."

"I hope it is a good sum this time," Scylla said while she burped vulgarly on the other end of the telephone. He could hear the sound of glasses. "I am getting tired of living in the shadows, doc... Sometimes I think about things, you know?"

"What do you mean?"

"You make millions there in Florida; you live like a king... I on the other hand receive the leftovers here," Scylla mumbled. "And all because of your fault... You ruined my face, doc. You fucked up my life." Then he heard another sound of glasses. "I wonder what the press would say if they knew that the great doctor Vinci also made mistakes..."

"Do not even dare to do such a thing," Vinci said feverish. "That would mean the end of me."

"Then you should better come with the money soon, doc. This time I do not want less than five big ones." Scylla hung up.

Vinci, the greatest plastic surgeon of all times, also hung up the pone in his elegant office in his clinic. Suddenly he felt that the great world he had created for himself was tumbling down. Laura Duncan wanted to investigate him and Scylla wanted to blackmail him. I could not allow it.

Francesco Vinci, or rather John Gravani, felt persecuted. The same as he had felt in his childhood, and in his rebellious youth. Once again, everybody wanted to finish him off, walk over him, take away his opportunity to exit... But they were not going to succeed. He had been able to arise from the misery and anonymity he used to live in with a lot of effort and pride. And nobody would ignore him evr again.

There was a solution for both his problems. The same solution he had for the beautiful although imperfect Nora Bardin. He would use the same solution for the nosy Laura and for Scylla… Death.

The world was already his, he said to himself. And nobody would take it away from him.

*   *

11

The American Airlines flight was just a few minutes away from his destination and for the Boeing to land on Mc Carran Airport in the city of Las Vegas.

Laura felt a shiver while she sat inside the cabin… She had a hunch she would find something very important for her investigation in that city. She thought about the fact that she had been so close to the reason she had sleepless nights, just the day before. She closed her eyes and remembered the appointment at vinci's Clinic.

*　　*

"How is the healing process of my face doing, Doctor?" Laura asked.

Francesco Vinci leaned toward her. His blue seductive eyes observed her in detail, without any hurry. He was just like an art dealer observing a splendid Italian Renascence painting.

"Satisfactorily," the surgeon answered. "Although I think the skin should be given a bit more stiffness under the cheekbones. The skin in that part of the face is the first one to loose elasticity during the aging process. This is easy to fix, and it is just so that the skin has a more natural look."

"Will I have to go into surgery again?"

"I think you will. I know that the patients do not really want to go back to the operating room so soon, but sometimes it is necessary." He stopped talking for a moment. "Do not worry, Miss Duncan. You will have the safety measures, as always."

Laura felt butterflies in her stomach. She would not have doubted Vinci's words a few weeks ago... However now, the situation was different. There were to many things about that surgeon to be doubtful about. On the other hand, Laura could not forget the great risks of facial reconstruction; blindness, brain damage and infection.

Hospitals and clinics are not unerring. It was risky anyway. Despite of the safety measures, accidents happened all the time. Her sister Sarah's death was the best example of medical negligence.

Vinci made her react when he asked her:

"Will you be in the city in case I would want to operate in a few days?"

Laura hesitated. She did not want Vinci to become suspicious of he distrust and her investigation.

"I am not very sure about that, Doctor," she answered. I have some things to do outside of Miami.

"Where? Very far from here?"

Laura hesitated again. Her next step was to go to Las Vegas. But she did not want the surgeon to know about that. She decided to lie:

"I have to go to Denver and see the possibility to have some concerts for the following year."

"Denver? That is a quiet city," Vinci said. "I have some friends there. The wives of cattle farmer." He smiled and then said: "Now show me your hands, I want to have a look at them."

Laura felt Vinci's thin hands holding hers. The same hands, she remembered, that had savagely hit a prostitute.

"The skin on your hands is healing perfectly," the great fraud smiled again.

* *

"I come to Las Vegas on holidays almost every year," an obese man, sitting next to Laura on the plane, said. "And what about you, miss? Are you on holidays too?"

"No," answered Laura.

"Is this your first time in this city?"

"Yes."

"This is a charming city, Miss. You will never get bored here. There are all kinds of entertainment."

Laura did not answer anything. Fun? She was not looking for that. The only thing she had in mind was to find anything interesting in that night club whose name was on the entrance Nora Bardin had.

The obese man smiled friendly and while he stood up from the seat in the Boeing, he pointed to an also obese woman, who was just trying to get up behind him. "My wife and I always stay in the same place; The Sahara on Freemont Street." He made a gesture with his enormous hand and said to Laura: "I would recommend you rent a car. That is the best way to go around the city and its sights."

It was around half past three in the afternoon when the passengers of the plane started to disembark. After the usual procedures on the airport, Laura took her lizard skin purse and went to the taxi stand.

She asked a taxi driver if he could take her to the Old Sand club. The driver nodded and Laura got inside the taxi.

The car drove away from Mc Carran Airport through Tropicana Avenue, and then it turned north and continued on Paradise Road. Inside the taxi, Laura contemplated the high buildings that belonged to the emblematic hotels and casinos of the city. They all looked equally impressive and were all on Las Vegas Boulevard. In day time, they looked insipid and a bit too extravagant, but at night time and thanks too the millions of neon lights they came to colourful life. Las Vegas was a city where you could the night. Laura thought that the gangsters who originally found it must have thought exactly that. It is the only place in the world where the horizon is publicity lights. It is a place that represents bets and the dream of easily winning millions of dollars. Las Vegas was founded on the basis of banality, excess and of ephemeral things. Luck is its engine; crime its reality. Laura imagined Elvis' ghost running around those intense streets that were the glory and the end of his legend.

The taxi stopped in front of a circular building whose design simulated the Roman Coliseum. There were some enormous palm trees at the entrance. The club did not look as one of the best. It must have been interesting some time ago, but now it looked out of fashion and repetitive. It looked like it needed a renovation.

Laura paid the taxi driver and got out of the taxi. She walked towards the entrance of the club. The place was closed at that time of the day, but she could see some people cleaning the rug in the entrance. On both walls there were posters of the shows that the club regularly offered. There also were numerous photographs of groups of dancers, choreographers, singers, musicians, etc.

Laura took her time to look at each of the faces of the dancers and the rest of the employees of the place. None of those faces were identical to hers. She was disappointed; but only a little.

One of the posters said that that the show in the Old Sand started at half past nine that evening. Laura thought she would come back later and see the show.

She took out a cigarette and lit it. She thought about the next step she would take in Las Vegas.

Nora Bardin had disappeared form Garden City almost six months ago, and Laura's theory was that if there was another woman that had received her same face features in Las Vegas that had been discovered by Nora, this new twin could have suffered the same fate as John Frank's daughter... Therefore the right parting spot was a list with all the photographs of missing people. However, Laura was hesitant to go to the police. She did not want to go to the authorities until she had something concrete to base a case on. And she did not have a legitimate reason to search around their files either.

So, she took Larry Wallace's advice. She got reference from him that would allow her to search the files of the Las Vegas Confidential newspaper. This was a weekly newspaper that covered news from the whole city, especially criminal and violent news. The Las Vegas Confidential happened to be owned by a friend of Wallace. They knew each other form the time Larry belonged to the red press in Los Angeles.

If a girl had gone missing in Las Vegas, the Confidential would probably have picked the story up. According to what Larry had told Laura, the offices of the newspaper were at the end of Charleston and its clipping library was completely computerized.

Laura put her sunglasses on before she went into the newspaper's building. She did not want anyone to recognise her appearance. If she found the photograph of a missing girl that looked just like her, she did not want any employee to remember both faces and establish any connection.

Larry's friend was a man around fifty years old. He was not tall and completely bald. He had a very red nose and wore a grey suit. His eyes were also grey, and looked a bit ironic and disenchanted. Just like the look of a looser. However, his laughter was nice.

"I am Ben Woodward," the man said as he stretched his hand.

Laura said her name and also stretched her short fingered-hand.

"Did Larry Wallace talk to you on the phone a couple of days ago?" Laura asked.

"Yes, he did," the bald man answered. "My old friend from California insisted about this favour and its confidentiality."

"That is right," Laura smiled.

"If I remember correctly, you wanted to visit our files about crimes."

"Yes. Especially about missing people," she said, without taking of her dark sunglasses.

"I see. Follow me."

"Laura followed him. They arrived at a small room that was painted blue and equipped with four personal computers. Laura asked for the files with information about recent years.

"No problem," Woodward said. "We have a computerised file with all the stories we have discovered about missing people, since a decade ago. Some cases are really moving."

Woodward opened a file that had many diskettes. He chose one that had the information that Laura needed and explained:

"Our system is able to show photographs on the screen." He inserted the diskette and taught her how to use the computer to find a particular case.

Laura learned how to work with the system very fast.

"Well, then I will leave you alone," the bald man told her. "I have some work to do."

"Thank you," Laura said. "I really appreciate this."

"Do not thank me," Woodward replied. "Thank Larry. I am just paying an old friend a favour. You know what? When we used to work together in the Santa Monica star my marriage failed and I started to have problems. It led me astray... I sunk into the world of alcohol and drugs, whores and gambling. I was introduced to hell. Do you understand? I fell into a dark hole and it was very difficult for me to get out. I was finished, on the edge of committing suicide... And then Larry appeared and gave me all of his support. I helped me through that horrible time." He stopped talking for a moment. His sweet smile appeared again. Then he continued: "Wallace is a good man. He is a bit stubborn and jealous sometimes, but he is a great man."

"I know," Laura answered.

Woodward pointed at her dark sunglasses.

"Maybe you should take those off. You would be able to see better. I do not understand the urge of some people to wear those things these days."

Laura did not reply. She surreptitiously turned towards on of the computers. When the bald journalist started to walk through the aisle, she closed the door and turned the lights off. She would work in the dark and only with the light of the computer screen. She sat down and now that nobody could see her, she took her dark sunglasses off.

She looked for news about missing people in the last three years.

She started to feel neglected and lost as she read the headlines on the computer screen. They were all sad stories that would make stir anybody's stomach. Most of the people were missing because it had been their choice. People that escaped, people that were disappointed in their marriage or of their jobs, some other people could not face their financial responsibilities, etc. The more she looked at the photographs and read the descriptions, the more she started to wonder where some of those people were and how their new lives were like.

Laura read for about two hours. Her eyes were beginning to feel sore and her neck ached. She had not found anything interesting yet. The clippings passed her eyes faster and faster.

After a while she found a clipping that was about the disappearance of a dancer... She started reading it:

"A twenty six year old woman," the same age she had, "disappeared two nights ago from the Old sand Club..."

Laura's heart started to beat faster. She nervously continued reading. "The dancer was called Patricia Plangman..." Then she read something... A phrase... She blinked... No... That could not be true...

She read the phrase again and again.

"The young dancer had recently undergone a plastic surgery."

Feeling completely desperate, Laura looked for a photograph...There wasn't any. She read the news article once again... Plastic surgery...

Laura continued reading trying to find more details about the Plangman case. She wondered if the case had been solved and where the woman was.

But she could not find any more about the case. Maybe the news was forgotten after a while and it had been replaced by other news.

Laura decided to move her legs. She stood up and put her dark sunglasses on again. She disconnected the computer and took out the diskette. Finally she left the room.

She returned the diskette to Mister Woodward and thanked him again.

Laura's heart was beating sp fast she could hardly breath.

She left the offices of the Las Vegas Confidential.

*   *

Once she was back on the street, she looked for a telephone booth and called to find out the address of the Missing Persons Department of the Las Vegas Police.

Shortly after that, Laura was sitting in Lieutenant Vincent Benitez' office. Lieutenant Benitez was in charge of the Missing Persons Department. The detective was middle aged, quite strongly built and he had an enormous black moustache. His eyes looked sleepy and soft. He seemed to be a simple and straightforward kind of man.

"Well the thing is, lieutenant." Laura started to stammer. She would have to make her questions tactfully. It was risky to go to police at this point. She had not wanted to do that, without having something more concrete. She took some breath and then continued. "It is a personal matter. It is about a very dear friend of mine and she has gone missing. I want to find her. As I told you, it is a personal matter. We know each other since we were little girls. Do you understand?"

The lieutenant nodded.

"The files are public, Miss Duncan," the detective said with a husky voice. "You or any other citizen that knows somebody, whether it is a relative or a friend, that has gone missing, has all the right in the world to be here." He cleaned his throat. "Give me the details about your missing friend."

"Her name is Patricia Plangman. She was a dancer at a night club."

"I have never heard about her."

"Well, I am sure you have a lot of cases..."

"Under what circumstances this person disappeared...?" Benitez asked putting a chewing gum in his mouth.

"She disappeared on her way home after working at the Old Sand night club, located north of Paradise Road. She disappeared about a year ago. Are you familiar with this club?"

The detective nodded. He closed his eyes and frantically chewed on his chewing gum. He thought in silence.

"Yes... I think I remember now," he finally said. "Although I am not personally familiarised with that particular case. That dancer had had a medical surgery, I think."

"Plastic surgery," Laura answered.

"Yes, that is it... Was she your childhood friend?"

"Yes."

"And what do you want to know?"

"I want to know if the case was ever solved and if she was ever found."

"I see," the lieutenant said. After a while, he continued, "I will go and get her file. Maybe you will find an answer there."

Laura felt the muscles on her face tighten while Benitez' thick fingers went through some old files, trying to find the correct name. Then the detective took one file in particular and put it on the desk. He sat down.

"Here it is…"

Laura noticed her throat was getting dry.

"Now," Benitez continued, "The conclusion of the case. Your friend had an accident, did you know that? Oh I suppose that is the reason behind the plastic surgery." He took a photograph that was inside the file and gave it to Laura. "Is this your friend?"

Laura's hands shook a little as she took the photograph. She saw the image of a young woman that was smiling… She did not look like her at all. Laura sighed. Then she though for a while and asked Benitez:

"Is there any photograph of her after the accident…?" Laura was struggling not to look too anxious.

"Let's see…" the lieutenant said. "I think so…" He looked through all the pieces of paper. He found another photograph. He looked at it carefully and then fixed his eyes on Laura. He looked at the photograph again. His teeth stopped chewing the chewing um. He pulled his eyebrows up and muttered: "Oh my God!"

"What is wrong…?" Laura asked.

"Oh dear! But what…? What is this all about, madam…? I…" Benitez walked towards Laura and took her glasses off. "Are you her twin or what?" He took the photograph and showed it to Laura. He was very irritated.

Laura felt panic and anxious because she had blown her cover. She leaned back in her chair and whispered. She took the photograph and looked at it with distrust… Maybe she had known what the photograph would show her all this time.

Yes, she had found another copy of herself. Another identical face. Another similar product of a perverted experiment performed by a disturbed mind…

It was the third copy she had discovered. How many more were there? The though alone made her shiver.

She slowly became serene. Her hands were still holding the photograph when she replied to Benitez:

"I am not her twin sister…"

"Aren't you?" the detective asked, while he chewed on the chewing gum. "Well, then, who are you? Some kind of clone? Maybe you are going to tell me you are some kind of close relative. Explain the situation to me a little, because I frankly do not understand anything."

"Look, lieutenant," Laura said. She nervously put her hand through her hair. "I will tell you the whole story in one moment… Let's say, my friend and myself, we both had plastic surgery and there were some coincidences…"

Benitez still seemed confused. He whistled.

"Damned… Are you serious madam?"

"Very serious, lieutenant." Laura assured him. "I guarantee that I will tell you all the details. But, you know what? I need to know how Patricia Plangman's case ended."

Benitez stared at her, feeling a bit reluctant and surprised. Then he realise that the attractive woman sitting in front of him and who had travelled from the other end of the country, was talking seriously and seemed serious about wanting some answers. The detective shook his head tiredly and looked through the file again. Laura though it took Benitez very long to move and turn every page while he chewed the chewing gum. He finally stopped at one page. He shook his head and pursed his frowned.

"It is not strange you lost contact with your twin friend." Benitez said.

"What do you mean?"

The police's face saddened.

"Miss Duncan," he mumbled, "Patricia Plangman is dead… For almost a year now… I am sorry…"

Laura sighed. She covered her face and tightened her knees. The chair shook a little.

"How did it happen?" she asked.

"I do not know," Benitez answered disappointed. "It does not say here. It just says she was found in the dessert, northeast of the city... The most part of her."

"The most part of her...?"

Benitez gave Laura a photograph of the case.

She lowered her sight to look at it. There, on a medium large photograph taken by the Las Vegas police, there was the body of a female.... That had been decapitated.

*   *

12

"You will not believe what I am just about to tell you," Laura told Larry.

She and Wallace were in Laura's kitchen again in Miami. Laura had come back from Las Vegas that afternoon and she had immediately called the journalist and artistic manager. Now they were both having a succulent bowl of spaghetti with champignons.

"Tell me already, honey." Wallace said.

Look," Laura started saying, "I have just found out that the great surgeon Francesco Vinci has created three identical faces. And that the owner of one of them, was found dead, without her head."

"Jesus!" Larry choked on the spaghetti.

"Now I know that Nora Bardin must have discovered the same thing. That is why she had the entrance to the Old Sand Club. The most pathetic thing is that Nora has disappeared and she has still not been found."

"Maybe her fate was the same as the girl from Las Vegas," Wallace suggested.

"That is what I think, Larry." Laura shuddered. "But, I can not really prove that Nora is dead. But it is a possibility. God!... And if she is dead, who else is too?" She gasped for some air. "Suppose that Vinci has a series of copies of faces and most of them are dead... What is going to happen to me?"

Wallace felt some shivers running down his spine. He finished his bowl of spaghetti and wiped his mouth with a napkin. Then he drank some cabernet and thought that Laura's theory made a lot of sense.

"Laura, I think it is time to go to the police," Wallace said.

She was not so sure about that. She had known Larry would suggest this. Wallace never joked around, when it came to the police. The journalist had some friends in the Miami Police Department that could help Laura. However, she was not very convinced. What would happen if the police made everything more complicated? What would happen if they made any foolish mistake and alerted Vinci? Everything she had found out would be useless. She looked at Larry:

"Your are right," she said, "but... let me think about it. Maybe I can discover something else..."

"I think you are getting involved in a serious business her, honey," Wallace said. "I think you should go to the police." He swallowed and then firmly added: "If you do not do it, I will."

"I just need a couple of more days," Laura asked.

"What for?"

"Just give me a couple of more days," Laura insisted. "Larry, trust me. My instinct has given me all that information up to now. I think I could do a lot more in a couple of more days."

Wallace did not answer. He did not like the idea of getting into an argument with Laura. In a certain way, he understood her curiosity and her urge to get to the bottom of this matter where she was the victim.

*   *

"I had to see you doctor Jung," Laura told the psychiatrist, the moment he opened the door of his office.

It was around ten o'clock in the morning when Laura arrived at Alan Jung's office on Biscayne Boulevard, next to the James L. Knight Centre. Laura had called the doctor asking to see him urgently. Jung told her to come immediately to his office.

The psychiatrist asked her to sit down and asked her:

"Has the visit anything to do with doctor Vinci, Miss Duncan?"

"Yes," Laura answered.

"Have you seen him?"

"No…" she hesitated. "I have found another of his patients that looks exactly like me."

Jung pretended not to understand.

"Exactly like you? I thought there was only one; that woman from Kansas who has disappeared."

"I will be completely honest with you," Laura said. "When I was here the last time, I did not mention that I had discovered something in the house in Garden City where the missing woman lived. That led me to another case…"

Jung looked at her full of doubt.

"Why didn't you tell me this before?"

"I needed to prove it," she answered.

"I see… This complicates the situation, doesn't it?"

"Of course it does," Laura assured. "Especially after I discovered that woman from Las Vegas is dead."

"Is… what?"

"She was found dead. Decapitated."

Jung felt as if he was getting kicked in his stomach. He tried to act normal though. He did not speak for a moment and then he said:

"That is horrible, Miss Duncan. Horrible... But you are not suggesting that doctor Vinci..."

"I do not know what I am suggesting. But that man gave these women the same face, and then something terrible happens to both of them. He is the only connexion between them."

Jung nodded. He sighed and walked towards the window of his office. It was a pleasant and sunny day outside. But the psychiatrist was shivering. He slowly turned in the direction of Laura.

"What are you going to do, Miss Duncan?"

"I am not really sure," Laura answered. "Maybe go to the police."

"I see." Jung reflected. "Well, that is what you should do, but... maybe you should wait."

"What for?"

Jung understood his world was falling apart. If Vinci went to jail, so would he. And that had to be avoided. He had to persuade that nosy woman somehow. I thought again. Then he said, with faked serenity:

"Because you could hurt a good man, a great professional in plastic surgery. Doctor Vinci could suffer irreparable damage to his career. It would destroy his reputation. And also in his life." He stopped talking for a while. He walked to where Laura was sitting. "Look, it could be a tragic coincidence... After all, the two women were not in identical situations. Anyway, I would not want to hurt someone intelligent and talented. Do you understand?"

Laura listened to him in silence. She thought that Jung was right n some way. She had to prove some other facts. Two more days would be enough... Laura was still convinced that she could trust the psychiatrist.

"All right, doctor." She said. "I will wait a little longer."

"I think that is the best you could do," Jung said. He then said cynically, "Please do not forget to keep me informed of whatever you find out. And if I think of something, I will call you." He tenderly took Laura's hand, like it was a father holding his favourite daughter's hand. Then he whispered: "And trust Francesco Vinci. He gave you the most beautiful face I have ever seen..."

Laura did not say anything. She just thought: "*Yes, a beautiful face, but not an exclusive one.*" She immediately thought about the small surgery Vinci had suggested. "*Would she put herself in the hands of that strange plastic surgeon again?*"

She could not find a definite answer for that.

*   *

The moment Laura had left the office, Jung grabbed the telephone. His hands were soaked in cold sweat, and shook. He started to feel an intense headache while he dialled the number.

"Francesco?" the psychiatrist said. "It's Alan Jung."

"Why are you calling me at this time, Alan? I am working." Vinci replied on the other side of the line.

"I am sorry to bother you, my friend," the psychiatrist said. "I am calling you to tell you that Laura Duncan was here. We are in trouble... She has been investigating things and she discovered the other woman with an identical face to hers. It is a dancer from Las Vegas that was found dead..." Then he started to get into more details about the conversation he had with Laura and asked Vinci: "How many women did you include in that experiment, Francesco?"

"What are you talking about?"

"You know very well what I am talking about, damned," Jung spat out the words. "How many more? You

promised me you would repeat it just once, un replicate…
But you lied to me!"

"Man, calm down. Calm down." Vinci said. "You
know that I will take care of everything. You just have to
keep on getting all the information you can from that
woman…"

"I will," Jung mumbled. "But I suggest you look for a
good rubber ring, because you are drowning, my friend."

"Yes, Alan, I guess you are right. But I would not
drown alone." Vinci replied and hung up. Vinci took his head
in his hands while he sat in his office. He felt like a rope was
tightening around his neck. Damned!

He stood up from behind his desk and walked through
his office thinking about the dancer from Las Vegas… *How
could they have found that lifeless body, if he had buried it in
the dessert?...He surely must have committed some kind of
mistake...* While he was thinking this, he said to himself:
"*Laura Duncan does not have any concrete proof that I was
involved in a crime, because I have been very careful about
the other murders.*" But he knew that if Laura opened her
mouth and publicly said everything she knew, it would cause
a wave of suspicions that would absolutely destroy his
reputation.

"*I should have gotten rid of that bitch earlier*" he said
to himself. Why hadn't he?... He had not found the right way
to kill her without raising any suspicions on himself. He had
to find a way!

He closed his eyes and listened to his heart beating
incessantly. He thought his experiment would be so brilliant
and perfect. He had dreamed of becoming an immortal plastic
surgeon, by creating an immortal face. Something like
Boticelli's Aphrodite, like the Mona Lisa, like the Venus de
Milo… A face that would be recognised in the entire world
for centuries… But, shit! Everything was getting screwed.

Maybe he had not been that brilliant after all. John
Gravani, the son of a house painter and the cook of a

restaurant had committed mistakes since his youth. He wondered why it was so hard to burry the past.

There is no tomorrow without a yesterday... But his yesterday was too despicable, that he had always wanted to change it. He had in some way...

He would kill Laura Duncan... Neither she nor anyone would take away his success.

He asked his secretary not to be disturbed for about an hour. He thought in his office, while a couple of grams of cocaine lightened his mind.

Some time later, he called his secretary again:

"Loretta, dear," Vinci's voice was calm again. "I have decided to schedule Miss Laura Duncan for a small surgery. Please, make the appointment as soon as possible."

"Of course, doctor."

"Tomorrow would be fine."

The secretary was disconcerted. "Doctor, your schedule is completely booked for the next three days..."

"It has to be tomorrow," Vinci insisted calmly. I have the feeling that Miss Duncan could have a slight skin infection."

*   *

13

The afternoon was pleasant and sunny. Laura was in the garden of her house listening to the singing birds, while she studied the music of Chopin. Suddenly the phone rang in her living room. Laura went inside the house. She thought that it was Wallace who had discovered something new; or maybe it was Doctor Jung with some new idea.

"Hello," Laura said.

At the other side of the line someone sighed deeply. Then there was silence.

"Who is this?"

Another sigh. After a few seconds, a female voice, that seemed a bit drunk and vulgar, asked slowly:

"Are you Laura Duncan...?"

"Yes. Who is this?"

"You... You." The voice seemed worried. It gave the impression that the person who owned that voice was going through a bad emotional moment in her life. "You were a patient of Doctor Vinci, weren't you?"

"Yes." Laura felt anxious. "Who are you?"

A new sigh. A bit longer this time. A deep sigh.

"I... I also was a patient of that monster," the drunken voice answered.

Laura felt as if her heart would stop beating.

"Nora?...Are you Nora Bardin...?"

On the other en d of the line, the vulgar voice did not answer for a moment. Then she answered she was not Nora Bardin.

"Then, who are you?" Laura insisted. "Please identify yourself!"

"My name is Scylla Dubois. You do not know me. I am from New Orleans... I think we need to talk."

"Why?"

"I have some information," the voice answered. She coughed and then continued: "some information that accuses that evil surgeon that ruined our lives..." She gave an address and said: "I will wait for you..." Then she hung up.

Laura watched the phone attentively without moving a muscle. She felt paralyzed, and barely felt her heart beating. Who was that women on the other side of the line? Another victim of Vinci atrocious experiment? Another copy of her face?

"God! How many other women were there with a similar face?" she wondered.

*   *

Laura knew that Larry Wallace would be very busy at his work at the Miami Globe. She called the journalist anyway, telling him that new details had come up in the investigation about Vinci. Wallace answered he would come round her house in a few hours.

Larry asked Laura to pour him a glass of red wine, while he heard about the strange telephone call from Louisiana.

"Jesus! This really turning into a horror movie, Laura," Wallace said after her heard everything. "Now, I am really convinced we should go to the police."

"I am going to New Orleans," Laura said, avoiding Wallace's advice to go to the police.

"All right," the journalist agreed. "Find that so called Scylla Dubois. I have no problem with that. But we are going to the police."

"Sure, we I come back from Louisiana."

"No, no, honey. Now. Soon. I do not think you understand the situation very well. If you go on, this matter can become dangerous."

She also drank a glass of Cabernet and answered firmly:

"I have a feeling that the police could screw everything up..."

Wallace sat down in the beach chair in the porch. He finished his glass of wine and asked Laura for another one. He agreed while he nodded.

"All right you win," he mumbled then. "I can not force you. Go to Louisiana. Find Scylla... But I am going to the police while you are gone. I do not want to be part of a crime. No."

She finished her wine and did not say anything, although she knew that Larry would do exactly as he had said he would.

*   *

Laura came out of the bathroom that was next to her bedroom. She had just taken a cold shower. She had around an hour before her flight to New Orleans. She was selecting the clothes she would wear on this trip, when, again, the phone rang. This time she answered in her bedroom.

"Miss Duncan?" a very pleasant and soft voice said.

"Yes, this is Laura Duncan." Laura answered.

"I am Loretta, from Doctor Vinci's clinic speaking. The doctor has gone through his file and he wishes you to undergo the small surgery that had been planned."

Laura had almost forgotten that detail. That proposal sounded extremely suspicious to her according to the circumstances. There you had a man with a questionable medical ethics, who she was investigating. Someone that could be a murderer. And he was asking her to place herself under his surgical knife. However, she was not supposed to act suspiciously.

"Oh..." she mumbled. "Is it urgent?"

"It is not dangerous, Miss Duncan," the secretary said. "The doctor thinks he should operate you as soon as possible to avoid future complications."

"I am really busy at the moment..." she started to make excuses for herself. "But I suppose it has to be done. I do not think I have any alternative. When will this be?"

"Tomorrow."

"That is impossible," Laura said. I have some engagements."

"The day after tomorrow, then?"

"No," Laura answered. "I need more time... Let's see, let's see." She thought for a moment. "I am free this Friday, how is that?"

Laura heard that the secretary on the other side of the line, softly talked to someone. It must be Vinci, she thought. Just a little while later, the refined voice of the best plastic surgeon in the world appeared on the other side of the line:

"Good afternoon, Miss Duncan. It's doctor Vinci."

She hesitated before she answered.

"Good afternoon, doctor."

"Do you know something?" the surgeon continued. "I would like to operate you as soon as possible, because I am afraid that you could suffer a postoperative infection." Vinci was actually boiling inside. He wanted to get rid of the obstacle called Laura Duncan as soon as possible, but he understood that if he pressured her, it would seem highly suspicious. He had to be tactful. He continued: "do you think, Miss Duncan? Cancel your engagements tomorrow, and check yourself in the clinic. It will be something very safe and fast."

Laura thought for a moment. She analyzed the best answer. Then she tightened all her muscles in her body, and firmly maintained her previous answer:

"I cannot before Friday, doctor. It's impossible," She answered. "I am just picking up my engagements after being absent for so long."

Vinci could hardly control his anger. He thought everything could explode before Friday; Laura could find strong evidence against him... Laura seemed to be resistant to the idea of the surgery... But Vinci knew how to handle the situation. He would accept her offer, because if Laura had irrefutable evidence before Friday, he would kill her outside the operating room.

He told her he accepted her offer.

A short moment after that, their conversation came to an end. Laura thought she was not really scared of putting herself in Vinci's hands. If he really was a murderer, he was also a really intelligent man and he would not do anything in front of other doctors or nurses.

She concentrated on her trip to New Orleans.

*   *

14

Wallace's friend who was a police officer was Sam Roth, and he was a lieutenant in the Homicide Brigade of the Miami police. He was a heavily built man, fifty three years old. His face looked tough and red; and his neck was a thick as that of a bull. He was an excellent police officer and had a great sense of humour. He sometimes liked to drink as a Cossack.

The piano bar where the journalist and the police officer met was called La Paloma. It was located in North Miami. Lieutenant Roth was the first one to arrive to the place, at around nine o'clock at night.

"Sit down Larry," the police officer said to Wallace, while he pointed at a chair. "Tell me what I can do for you."

"It is about a friend of mine; Laura Duncan," Wallace started to say after he had ordered a glass of brandy. "She is a very special person for me."

"I have seen her photograph in the magazines," Roth said, while he drank his second dry martini. "She is pianist, right?"

"Yes, she gives excellent concerts. She tours all around the country."

Roth nodded. Then he smiled and he winked.

"She is also very beautiful," he said. "Since when have you been sleeping with her, my friend?"

"I have known her for a couple of years," Wallace said smilingly. He tasted his brandy and started to tell his friend everything. "Well, Laura suffered a horrible accident. Her face was completely ruined and it had to be reconstructed. Plastic surgery, I mean. Do you understand me? The outcome was unbelievable, she looked amazing. Much more attractive than she was before... I won't tell you too many details... But after the surgery she discovered something... the doctor who made
her new face, had also given that same face to two other women."

Roth nodded again, without showing a lot of interest. He finished his martini. Larry asked another glass and continued saying:

"My friend Laura started to investigate about the other women. Anyone one in her position would do the same..." Larry stopped smoking for a minute.

"Go on, dude. I am listening to you," Roth mumbled as he wetted his lips with a new martini.

"Until now, Laura has found one of the women that had disappeared, and the other has been murdered. And now she is looking for a third woman."

"Is your friend a pianist or a police officer?" the lieutenant joked around.

"She is actually a really persistent pianist sometimes," Wallace replied smilingly. "She wants to know the reason behind the things that plastic surgeon does."

"I see." Roth finished his third martini. "Go on, duded."

"One of the women was from Kansas, the other was form Nevada, and the third one is probably from Louisiana." He stopped talking for a moment. "Laura is now going there, as we speak, to investigate the matter more closely."

"All those cities are not my territory, dude," Roth said.

"I know. But that doctor, the plastic surgeon, Francesco Vinci, lives here in Florida, Palm Beach. Laura thinks that he is involved in the disappearances and the murder."

"Why?"

"The guy is a bit weird..." Wallace answered. "Just think about the fact, that he has given the same face to four different women! Normal plastic surgeons would not do something like that. That is unethical... almost perverse."

"This country is full of weird and crazy people," the lieutenant commented disregarded.

Wallace thought that Roth was right. He asked for another round of drinks.

"Will you help me Sam?" he asked a second later.

"I will investigate that guy, that so called Francesco Vinci, if that is what you want," The detective answered, while he drank he fourth dry martini. "I will make some phone calls to Kansas and Nevada. I know some people there. If that surgeon is up to something bad, I will know about it."

"All right," Wallace said. He looked at his watch and added: "Sam, my friend; Laura Duncan is very special to me... And you know what? I fear for her safety... Sometimes I think she is taking too many risks."

"Do you want me to get some of my men to watch over her?"

"That is precisely what I want."

"Well, consider it done, Larry." Roth slowly tasted his martini, like it was going to be his last.

*   *

It was dark and hot as a stove in the city of New Orleans. Laura had arrived have an hour ago, in an American Airlines Flight. Now she was standing in the middle of Bourbon Street, the most popular street of the French Quarter, the neighbourhood where the city had been founded.

She opened her elegant purse and took out a handkerchief. She dried the sweat of her forehead. She felt her armpits soaked in sweat. Damned! The sweat would ruin her fine Italian design blouse. She though and tried to remember Scylla Dubois' words: "...*Look for me at the end of Bourbon Street, in the Magnolia Club, after ten o'clock...*"

Laura started her search again, and looked at the bars and restaurants of the street. She could hear jazz music coming from inside them. The music got mixed with the typical noise clients of bars and clubs make. There were people of all kind of colours and races going from one side of the street to the other. The French Quarter had a special flavour to it at night.

Laura kept on walking and searching for the Magnolia Club. Finally she found a small notice board that the club was at the end of a side alley, which was dark and desolated.

Laura went down the alley. Slowly she walked away from Bourbon Street.

The club was small, sombre and vulgar. She listened to a choking voice that sang. Then she could hear the sound of glasses and laughter. She went in the club. That place was not at all elegant. A dense tobacco smoke floated in the air. An alcohol stench came from the walls. There were not many clients, and almost all of them were drunk. This must bee Scylla Dubois' environment.

The voice that was singing belonged to an awfully dressed little man. He was bald and standing on a wooden stage at the back of the club.

Laura found the environment horrible. She did not want to stay in that place too long. She walked towards the bar and asked for Scylla Dubois. The employee looked at her. His eyes immediately showed surprise and he said:

"Are you're her sister, or what...? You look identically like her!"

"I am a friend," Laura answered. "Where is she?"

The club's owner smiled ironically. He pointed at the stage where the awfully dressed little man was still imitating Sinatra.

"She comes after Benny," he answered. "She appears in the snake act." He twisted and turned his body joking around. "You will have to wait."

Laura nodded. She thought about ordering a glass of gin; but then she hesitated and just asked for a glass of water.

She sat at an empty table in a corner. The minutes went so extremely slow, it seemed a torture. Laura looked around the decadent club, and thought that this investigation about Vinci had made her visit some unbelievably dark places.

Finally the awfully dressed little man disappeared from the stage. The voice off-screen said: "now, ladies and gentleman, the Magnolia club is happy to present Scylla and the serpent..."

The few people in the audience hardly clapped.

All the lights were turned down, except the ones that lit up the wooden stage. At the same time some drums started to sound.   An extremely thin young travesty appeared on stage. He was wearing a dress with some feathers and danced around in circles as a large python was curled around his neck. He was wearing a mask that covered his face.

Laura was astonished... Scylla Dubois was not a woman, but a man... '*Had Vinci given her face to a homosexual?*' she wondered. Her question would only be answered when the man on the stage took of his mask... But if that travesty was another copy of her face, she thought, it would only prove that the surgeon had gone too far in his so called 'experiment'.

How many people had Vinci involved in his sinister plan?

Laura choked when she was finishing her glass of water. She could not avoid feeling the desire to light a cigarette. And so she did.

She kept on waiting, blaming herself for being in that place.

Twenty minutes later, the travesty finished his act with the serpent and disappeared from the stage while the audience screamed some rude things. The lights of the place were turned on.

Laura stood up from her table and noticed the man at the bar looking curiously at her. She stormed to back of the club and followed the travesty. She saw he opened one of the doors in a hall and went inside.

Laura shyly knocked on the door. Nothing. She knocked again. On the other side of the door she heard a voice saying:

"What do you want...?"

"I am Laura Duncan," Laura answered. "You called me..."

She heard some steps inside the room. Then the door opened and the man appeared. He was still wearing the mask, but the python around his neck had disappeared. The travesty nodded and slowly took of the mask. It seemed a lightening flashed through his dark eyes.

However, Laura was even more surprised. She was out of breath when she saw his face in front of her. It was as if she was looking in a mirror... She went from feeling astonished to feeling horrified in silent... The travesty's face was identical top hers, except for a nasty scar on one of his cheeks. It seemed a scar caused by a knife.

"Doctor Vinci ruined my face, Miss Duncan..." the man said later.

His voiced sounded very feminine and vulgar, Laura thought. On the phone anyone could have been confused. Laura was silent for a second and then asked him:

"How did you find out about me, Scylla?"

"That is simple," the man answered. "I saw a photograph of you in the magazine of Vinci's clinic. I almost died when I saw you! I understood that Francesco was still up to his immoral activities. That is when I decided to get in touch with you."

"What do you mean by 'immoral activities'?" Laura asked.

"That is the information I have and that I told you about over the phone."

"What kind of information?"

"Names, addresses, photographs... of five identical faces, including you and me. Unbelievable, isn't it? Not only we have the same identical face, Miss Duncan."

This was something Laura already knew, although a question raised in her head: 'who was the fifth face?'

"How did you find out about all of this, Scylla?" she mumbled a second later.

The man lit a cigarette and put it between his yellow teeth. He looked at Laura and answered:

"I will tell you. I have everything in my room."

"So, let's go to you room," Laura suggested.

*   *

"Whisky?" Scylla offered.

Laura nodded. They both were in a small room on St. Charles Avenue, next to the Lafayette cemetery. The room was very untidy and smelled of sweat, alcohol and other horrible things. A disgusting unmade bed, a table and some old chairs were the only furniture the room had. Laura wanted to get the meeting with Scylla over with as soon as possible.

The man poured a glass of whisky for Laura and himself. He sat on a chair and invite Laura to do the same. Scylla coughed heavily and then she drank some whisky. He started to explain everything to Laura.

"I was in jail in New Orleans, charged of theft and some other minor crimes. I had stolen some things here and there. Inside the prison, some of the prisoners were always annoying me, but I did not pay any attention to them, in spite of the mocking. The one day I got involved in a fight. A brutal fight... I received the worse part; they hit my face with bottles. It was horrible!... I thought I was never going to have a normal face ever again." He stopped talking and drank some whisky. "Then, when I was in hospital, I was lucky enough that the best plastic surgeon in the country, Francesco Vinci, included me in his programme free surgeries. I did not spend a dime on the reconstruction of my face... at the beginning, when the doctor had given me this fabulous face, I thought that Vinci was some kind of saint, that he was my saviour. Just a short while later, my new face started to show some problems in the scaring process of one of my cheeks... That son of a bitch had committed some mistake and ruined my face!... I got terribly frustrated... And I started to get suspicious of Vinci and his magical knife. Scylla looked at Laura, just as if he was looking in a mirror. "I investigated the doctor. I could break into his office here in this city, and have a look at the files he had there, and I discovered some things..." he stopped talking and finished his drink.

"What did you discover, Scylla?"

The travesty left the empty glass next to him and stood up from the chair. He took a shoe box from under his bed. He had a file inside and gave it to Laura. She looked through it.

She found the medical records and the photographs of the faces of Nora Bardin and Patricia Plangman. There also were photographs of before and after the reconstruction of their faces. She found her own medical record as well. Besides all of this information she found the medical record and photographs, front and profile, of a fifth face. Laura had never seen this face before. The girl on the photographs seemed to be around twenty five years old. On the back of the photographs were two words written: 'January – Dallas'.

"Interesting information, don't you think?" Scylla said.

Laura nodded, and wiped the sweat on her forehead with a handkerchief. Then she asked:

"How did you get all of this?"

"I stole it ..." Scylla's voice was still sounded very feminine and that confused Laura a little. The man continued speaking. "You, me and those other three people were all Vinci's patients, and for some strange reason we received the same face... And the worst part of all of this is that the other three are missing."

"At least one of them has been found," Laura replied. "Patricia Plangman from Las Vegas was found in the dessert...she had been decapitated."

Scylla looked at Laura with her mouth wide open. She took a deep breath.

"Are you serious?"

"Of course I am. That girl is dead..."

"How did you know...?"

"Because I have done my own research related to Vinci and the series of faces."

Scylla, still feeling very surprised, swallowed some saliva. She nervously ran her fingers through her dirty long hair.

"Do you think Vinci is involved in that murder?"

"He probably is. That is the most logical hypothesis, don't you think? That man is a pervert." Laura clenched her wrists around the records. She remembered Sarah's death, caused by medical negligence, again. She though that some of the doctors were sly criminals. Then she asked Scylla:

"Why haven't you gone to the Police with all of this?"

"Because, I would run no chance against the distinguished and wealthy doctor Vinci. Who would believe somebody like me? My criminal record is quite big..." The dancer stopped talking for a moment. "That is why I called you, Laura..."

"What do you mean?"

"A person like you is believable."

Laura knew that Scylla was right.

"All right," she said as she raised the medical records, which were still clenched in her wrists. "I will give this information to the Police."

Scylla looked at her in a strange way.

"What is wrong?"

Scylla hesitated. She ran her fingers through her hair again. She knew the moment had arrived to get some money out of that elegant lady from Miami, just the way she got out of Vinci.

"Laura...," she started to mumble cynically. "I... I need something in return for that... information. Do you what I mean?"

"Money."

Scylla nodded, without looking at Laura's face.

Laura looked reluctant. She had not imagined such a request.

"How much?"

"Five thousand dollars would deal the deal."

Laura thought about the whole situation for a moment. What kind of dirty game was all of this? Scylla wanted to take revenge of Vinci, but she also wanted her money. She wondered if that would be the first and only request for money Scylla would make. There probably would be more. Laura thought about the request again. Then she decided to leave the medical records on the table.

"You know what, Scylla? I think I will have think about all of this for a while. I will call you at the Magnolia in a few days. Now it is time for me to leave."

Scylla did not say anything, but looked very disappointed.

*   *

15

"Scylla Dubois turned out to be a homosexual," Laura told Wallace.

Just as the other times, it was already becoming darker in the south of Florida, and they were both in the kitchen in Laura's house. This time they were eating ice-cream with strawberries.

"And her face was identical to mine," Laura continued saying. "Although she had an ugly scar on one of her cheeks. Something must have gone wrong in Vinci's surgery."

"I see," said Wallace. He mixed a little bit of ice-cream with some cabernet Laura had and which he liked so much. Then he said: "You mentioned that that travesty asked for some money in return for the medical records."

"That is right," Laura answered. "But I have not made up my mind about that yet. It all seemed a little suspicious to me. Maybe Scylla wants to get some money out of me, using the whole Vinci affair as an excuse. The travesty is a poor

dancer who stole the medical records from the office
Vinci has in the New Orleans Hospital. The medical records
are of the same people I had been investigating, except of a
fifth person, who I did not know about."

"A fifth patient?" Wallace wrinkled his forehead.
"There is a fifth face?"

"Yes. I do not know who it is; I just saw a photograph among
the other medical records. It is an attractive young woman, of
around twenty five years old. On the back of that photograph,
there were only two words written: 'January – Dallas'."

"I will ask Lieutenant Roth to investigate Vinci's
activities sin Texas." Wallace shook his head disappointedly.
"I would bet you, we are going to find another mysteriously
missing girl. And even worse than that; it could be that the
girl from Dallas is already dead…"

"Probably, she is." Laura admitted.

Wallace finished his ice-cream with cabernet and
thought for a while.

Then he said to Laura:

"Considering the fact that all the missing girls are also
dead…we could speculate that all of the five patients received
an identical face, and that only you and the dancer from
Louisiana are still alive." He looked at Laura. "Have ever
wondered why, honey?"

Laura had. But she had not been able to come up with
a reasonable answer.

"I do not know, Larry."

Wallace became very tense and said:

"Maybe Vinci is planning something for you and
Scylla."

"Vinci is capable of anything," Laura said.

"I am warning you again, honey," Wallace raised his
voice. "Be careful and keep you eyes wide open. The last
thing I want is to go to your funeral.

*   *

Vinci's sensitive hands were performing the last stitch on the reconstructed face of little nine year old Christine. She had been bitten by a dog in the middle of her cheeks. The surgeon ordered the nurse to put bandage on girl's face and he took off his surgical gloves and his red coat.

Vinci left the Operating Room, thinking about the fact that Christine was a girl that came from a poor suburb in the city. Her parents could not have been able to pay for a surgery like that. But he had agreed on doing that for free.

Sometimes, he enjoyed being kind-hearted with other people. However, some people were ungrateful with his services… He remembered Laura Duncan and felt rage… That distrustful and nosy pianist would receive what she deserved very soon. She had actually had less than forty eight hours to live. He thought it was unbelievable that she would still put her self voluntarily under his surgical knife, even after she had been investigating about the identical faces…

He went to his office.

A short while after that, he looked at one of his favourite original paintings. He had bought it in an auction in Paris and it hung on the wall of his office. It was a naked woman painted by the talented Modigliani.

He softly took the painting of the wall and left it on the table. Behind the place the painting had been hanging, there was a safe in the wall. Vinci opened it.

He wrapped his right hand in a handkerchief and took a little bottle out of the metal box. The little bottle contained a powerful and colourless poison.

Vinci looked at the bottle for a long time and then put it back in the box, thinking he would inject a dose of that poison into Laura just at the end of the surgery. The poison acted very quickly especially affecting the nervous system and the brain. She would die in less than two hours. Maybe she would suffer a general paralysis…

'*Goodbye Laura Duncan,*' he said to himself. '*You should have never messed with me…*'

He hung the Modigliani on the wall. He suddenly felt tired, somewhat anxious and depressed. He always felt depressed when he had to kill one of his patients. But he tried not to pay more attention to it as it was necessary. He understood that the depression was common in artists and geniuses who had high goals in their lives.

He stepped towards his desk. He unlocked one of the drawers and opened it. He frantically inhaled a bit of cocaine. The anxiety immediately disappeared and he felt more relieved and vital.

He looked at the time on his Cartier watch. It was twenty past eight in the evening. He grabbed his phone on his desk. The phone rang a couple of times before someone answered it on the other side.

"Miss Duncan?"

There was a long silence at the other side of the line.

"Doctor Vinci…" Laura's voice sounded surprised.

"Yes. I hope I am not interrupting something important. I was calling you to remind you that you have to admit yourself into my clinic first time this Monday. I guess you remember?"

"Of course I remember, doctor. I will be there."

"I am glad to hear that Miss Duncan. How is your face doing? Have you felt the tightness again?"

"It is getting less."

"And what about your hands? Have you played piano as easy as you did previously?"

"Yes," Laura lied.

"That is fantastic." Vinci was silent for a moment. "What about your emotional state? Is there something that is bothering you?"

Laura hesitated a little.

"No," she lied again.

"Are you still seeing Doctor Jung?"

"Yes."

"He is an excellent psychiatrist," Vinci said. "He is the best in the state of Florida."

"That is true," Laura agreed. "Doctor Jung has helped me a lot."

"And how is your social life doing?"

"Fine."

"Any trips?"

"Some…" Laura hesitated again. She did not want to give anything about the investigation she was doing, away to that guy.

"I am glad, Miss Duncan," Vinci said. "I will not take anymore time from you. Good Night."

"Good night, doctor."

*   *

Wallace called Lieutenant Roth the next morning. They agreed on meeting again in the piano bar called La Paloma.

"What is all this about, old friend," Roth asked as he drank his first dry martini of that day.

Wallace sat down next to the table of the lieutenant Roth, with a glass of liquor in his hand. He started to fill the lieutenant in on the details of the recent discoveries of Laura in Louisiana; the fifth patient of Vinci with and identical face.

Roth listened silently while he drank and nodded his head. He finally said, without showing a lot of interest:

"Did you say Dallas, old friend? That is way out of my territory…But I will see what I can do."

"I need you to do the best that you can, Sam." Wallace insisted. "It is possible that the young woman from Dallas is missing and dead. What you are able to discover in that Texan city could be vital to accuse Francesco Vinci of homicide."

"I see," the lieutenant said. "I will make some phone calls to the Police Department in Dallas. I will tell you everything I find out tonight."

Wallace smiled pleased as he held his glass which was almost empty.

"Thanks again for your help, Sam."

The lieutenant shrugged his shoulders.

"You are welcome, my friend. Now, let's asked for another round of drinks."

• *

16

Vinci parked his Lamborghini in the garage of his elegant house after returning from the annual plastic surgeons convention of the state of Florida held in the distinguished Vizcaya Palace. On that occasion the annual convention had been significantly special for him, because he had received an important price for his progress in the plastic surgery on burned patients. This meant the work he had performed to reconstruct Laura Duncan's face.

He had given her a new and beautiful face to that wretched girl. And how had she paid him back? Investigating about him, sniffing around his work... That ungrateful bitch! He burst into his house. He took off his elegant white jacket and walked towards the bar in the living room. He served himself a glass of whiskey on the rocks. While drank it he felt proud of himself for receiving that price. Another success in his professional career.

The rebel John Gravani had never imagined he would come so far.

The phone on the crystal table rang a couple of times. Vinci answered thinking it was a surgeon colleague that was calling to congratulate him for the important price he 'had received.

"It is me, doc," Scylla mumbled on the other side of the line.

"Hearing her voice was like a bucket of cold water for Vinci. The least he wanted was to hear that horrible human being's voice on that glorious evening.

"How did you get my home telephone number?" the surgeon said. "It is a secret number that does not appear in any phonebook. I do not recall giving it to you."

"I fooled you secretary, doc. I told her I was your sister."

"I do not have any sisters, damned." Vinci replied.

"I know," Scylla said. "But your secretary does not know that."

Silence.

"What do you want?" Vinci asked a second later.

"The same as always," Scylla answered. "Money. When are you coming to see me?

"I am very busy right now…"

"Have your forgotten your medical mistakes, doc?"

"No, I have not. You will just have to wait a little while…"

"Wait? I am tired of waiting, you son of a bitch," Scylla answered vehemently. "I am sure you never make your wealthy and famous patients wait for you… including that lovely Laura Duncan."

Vinci was perplexed. His voice hardly came out of his mouth when he asked:

"What did you say? What do you know about Laura…?"

Silence.

"I talked to her, doc... But do not worry, I did not tell anything about us."

"Damned. Why did you do that?"

"I guess, I wanted to meet my twin," Scylla joked around. "But, calm down, I did not tell her anything... Although I maybe will if I do not receive any news from you... You should better come and visit me, and bring a big present, you know what I am talking about."

Vinci was on the edge of rage. He could not trust Scylla Dubois anymore. He had to get rid of her as soon as possible. That homosexual had become a time bomb! He had to stop her! The great plastic surgeon faked to be serene and clam. He looked at his Cartier watch. It was almost eleven o'clock at night. I thought he could take his private jet and fly to Louisiana. He would take care of the problem before dawn.

"All right,"

He surgeon said. "I will fly to new Orleans tonight. Wait for me at the usual place."

"I will be there, doc," Scylla answered. Then she hung up.

*   *

At the same moment Vinci finished talking to Scylla Dubois, the phone started ringing in Larry Wallace's bedroom, in West Miami.

Wallace was in the bathroom, next to the bedroom, taking his usual nightly shower.

The phone rang four times. Larry heard it and quickly got out of the shower. He wrapped a towel around his wet body in a towel and went to the bedroom. He picked up the phone:

"Larry?"

Wallace immediately recognised Lieutenant Sam Roth's voice on the other side of the phone. He also recognised the sound of glasses.

"Hello, Sam. Tell me."

He heard the sound of glasses again.

"There is something really wrong in Dallas regarding to that plastic surgeon, old friend," the lieutenant said.

"What did you find out, Sam?"

"My friends in Texas went through Vinci's records in that city. He has performed surgery on half a dozen people, mostly women. But listen to this: the medical records, their photographs included, have disappeared."

"Disappeared?" Wallace asked. "How can they have disappeared?"

"If Vinci wants them to disappear, they disappear," Wallace answered himself. "The guy has destroyed the evidence. He is apparently very careful with the things he does. We are in trouble, man. What can we do?"

Roth thought on the other side of the phone.

"Do you know what?" the lieutenant said after a while. "I am thinking about going to Texas tomorrow. I will go and investigate the disappearance of those young women in Dallas myself. I am realizing that that surgeon has been doing some illegal things."

"Good luck over there, Sam," Wallace said.

*   *

17

Scylla's dilapidated Volkswagen parked in the desolated jetty. The dancer got out of the car and walked towards the wooden pier. She lit a cigarette and contemplated the serenity of the waters of Lake Pontchartrain.

Scylla looked around her. The night was very nice and there was nobody else around. She loved the night; to work and wander around in the shadows. This way, the rest of the people hardly noticed the imperfections on his face... Which was the fault of that bastard!

It was around one o'clock in the morning, and Vinci would soon arrive to the place where they had been meeting for the past three years. Scylla finished her cigarette and lit another one.

She waited impatiently. She really needed Vinci's money desperately...She suddenly heard steps on the grass at her back. Scylla turned around and saw the plastic surgeon. She actually saw a black figure, but it smelled like Vinci; as his expensive perfume.

"Hello doc," the dancer mumbled. "Did you bring my money?"

Vinci nodded his head. He took something out of the pocket of his jacket.

"Here it is," he groaned.

Scylla took the envelope and walked towards the car. She lit the front lights of the Volkswagen. She immediately stopped in front of them and started to count the money inside the envelope.

"There is only one thousand dollars here, doc," she moaned.

Vinci walked towards the dancer and said:

"I will give you the rest if you tell me exactly what you said to that woman."

"Do you mean Laura Duncan?"

"You know I mean her," Vinci answered. What did you mention to that bitch...?"

Scylla shook her head.

"I did not tell her anything important, Johnny. It was a short chat, nothing else."

"Do not call me Johnny... I am Francesco Vinci."

"To me you are always going to be Johnny Gravani, my childhood friend from the Bensonhurst neighbourhood in Brooklyn. The arrogant little boy that dreamed about becoming a great artist. At least you are a great sculptor of flesh..." She smiled ironically. It only happens that you have become a little insane half way to fame and fortune, my friend..."

"Shut up! Vinci screamed and insisted, "What the hell did you tell Laura?"
"I already told I told her nothing. I just wanted to see her. I wanted to check how identical our faces were."

Vinci did not ask his old friend anything else, but he knew Scylla was lying. He had probably given Laura the information in exchange for some money... He hated Scylla. He felt his long time friend had betrayed him... And to think they knew each other since they had been children. He nostalgically remembered when they had been ten years old, and they used to masturbate together in the school bathrooms... However, things had changed now. Vinci, blinded by his selfish success, did not feel anything towards Scylla Dubois. The dancer had become an obstacle in his raise to success.

"Here is the rest of the money," Vinci said as he threw another envelope towards Scylla.

The dancer caught the envelope in the air. She stood in front the car lights again and started counting the money inside the envelope.

Vinci sneaked behind Scylla. Then he covered his hands with some surgical gloves, to avoid getting dirty with the dancer's blood... Then he took out the surgical knife.

Laura Duncan could not get any sleep on the early Friday morning. Vinci's secretary had called her some hours before, to tell she had to be admitted in the clinic around eight o'clock in the morning.

Laura finished packing the bag she was taking to the clinic, and decided she was going to call her friend Larry Wallace.

The journalist wished her all the best in the surgery, and told her that Sam Roth had discovered some irregularities in the medical files of Vinci in Dallas. That was way he would travel to that city that following Friday to investigate the issue. Wallace promised he would tell Laura the results about Roth's research as soon as possible.

*   *

18

That Friday at the end of June, Sam Roth arrived at the Police Department in Dallas, just before ten o'clock in the morning.

To help him with his investigation, the police men in Dallas had assigned him a young sergeant, named Smith. He accompanied Roth to a small room were there only was a table and an electric fan that was working at its maximum speed because the heath in Dallas was as terrible as it was in Florida. The room was located next to the file section of the department.

Smith already knew what information the lieutenant from the Homicide Department in Miami was interested in. He showed him a number of photographs taken of crime victims. Although Roth had specifically asked Dallas any information about any murder victim found decapitated, his request had been lost in the middle of burocracy. Smith only knew that Roth was looking for a victim that had been "raped" and that that victim's face was physically very similar to that of a young pianist in Miami, whose photo the lieutenant had.

In the last two years there had been 58 victims of murders that had been cut into pieces or raped. On Roth's request, the photographs and files belonging to all 58 cases were given to him.

Most of the files contained a photograph. Some of them did not. He realised very quickly that none of those photographs looked like Laura Duncan.

"Maybe the woman is still alive, lieutenant," Smith commented to Roth, while both of them went through the files.

Roth nodded disappointedly. He realised that if he did not find some kind of evidence there in Dallas as soon as possible, he could not charge Vinci with murder as Wallace and his friend wanted. Up to that moment, the only thing he was sure of was that Francesco Vinci was an eccentric plastic surgeon; that he was not very ethical in his procedures and that he created identical faces.

Roth wiped his sweaty face with a handkerchief and looked at his watch. It was almost noon. He felt emptiness in his stomach and realised he need to eat something and drink a lot of glasses of whisky quickly. He needed a smoke too. He put his thick hand on Smith's shoulder and said:

"Let's leave this for a moment, man. I will buy you lunch. We can continue looking through the files this afternoon."

*   *

Three hours before Roth arrived to Dallas, Laura Duncan was checking herself into the clinic to start the preparations for her surgery.

Laura was given the best room of the clinic. It was the same room the wife of a very well-known Californian magnate had used a couple of days earlier. While she waited for the nurses, she found out that her surgery was planned for twenty past eleven that morning. She would get operated by a group of resident doctors; if she did not oppose to that. She finally told the nurse that gave her the forms to fill, that she did not have any problems with that. She thought that the more witnesses there were, the safest it was.

Vinci came to say hello to her. He was wearing his usual red robe and a cap of the same colour. It made him look like a catholic cardinal. The doctor was carrying the bottle of deathly poison that would kill Laura Duncan in one of his pockets...

A few minutes after Vinci's visit, nurse Anderson came into the room. Laura remembered her from her previous surgeries in the clinic. Anderson was a nice and friendly person around Laura's age. They had had a good understanding during the previous surgeries de pianist had had.

Laura had no idea that according to Francesco Vinci's perverted plan, tha smiling nurse would inject the poison into Laura's body...

"I want you to take these pills," Anderson told Laura. "One every half an hour. We will come and get you twenty minutes before the scheduled surgery time. The surgery is scheduled to finish twenty minutes to two in the afternoon. That is when you will be returning to your room. It is not a major surgery, but the doctor likes to explain everything to his students."

"I understand," Laura said. She hesitated for a moment and then asked: "Did you get these pills yourself?"

The nurse looked at her. She seemed curious about the question.

"Of course...Sure I did. I check the medicine regularly. Why?"

"I was just wondering. I am bit nervous, I guess."

"There is nothing to be nervous about. We are a good team. Everything is under control. There aren't any risks."

Laura did not say anything.

At the same moment she was talking to the nurse, Vinci was walking through the halls at the back of his clinic. He was going towards the cellar were they kept all the medicines. He knew he would not find anybody there at that time of the day. All the cupboards would be closed and all the alarms on in case of a robbery. As he knew the codes he unlocked and deactivated everything without any problems.

He quickly took a real liquid based on magnesium and adenosine out of the cupboard and replaced it with the poison he had in his pocket. He changed the etiquettes on the bottles as well. Both liquids were identical.

*   *

"I think I found something..." Roth said, while he went through the file of a murder victim. The head was missing. She had been murdered at night and the body had been found hidden between some bushes in a ravine.

"Al right," the sergeant answered, less enthusiastic. "But we have already found two other files where the head also had been missing. He photographs do not match the photograph you brought form Miami.

"There are no photographs here," Roth said.
Smith did not answer for a second, and thought about what that meant.

"Well, that changes things. Why don't you think there are any photographs?"

"Oh..." Roth wiped the sweat of his forehead again with the handkerchief. "There are many reasons why in a case like this, there are no photographs. I mean, maybe they could not get any photographs from the family because there wasn't any family. Maybe they did not take any because…well, because there was no head…so therefore, there is no face."

Smith half-closed his eyes.

"What will we do?"

Roth kept going through the file.

"I have a feeling that this might be what I have been looking for. Let's see, let's see…the same age as the victim… But there is nothing about the family or friends… She was a loner." He went through the sheets of paper again. "Listen, the forensic record says she was stabbed in the heart with something that had a very sharp cutting edge, probably a surgical knife…Damned! Who use surgical knives? Doctors, surgeons…"

Smith got a little more enthusiastic.

"What personal information do we have of this woman…?"

"She worked as a waitress at a bowling centre on First Avenue," Roth answered. "…it says here she suffered a very severe accident at home; a gas explosion in the kitchen of the house rented…" The muscles on the lieutenant's face got very tense. Then he said: "We have to go and pay that bowling centre a visit. I have a feeling about this young woman."

*   *

In Palm Beach, hundreds of miles away from Dallas, Doctor Vinci was talking to his students:

"Ladies and gentlemen," the surgeon announced with his fine voice. "Let me introduce you to a great and very charming lady; Laura Duncan. She is one of my favourite patients and a fabulous pianist. She gives concerts all over the country. You surely must have heard about her before. Some time ago, Laura had a terrible accident that ruined her face. It was a horrible experience for her... But thanks to plastic surgery, I can proudly say, I was able to give her back this face... Please say hello to her, ladies and gentlemen."

A wave of applause filled the room. Vinci always did the same thing; let the patient receive the applause of the audience there to watch the surgery.

"How are you feeling, Miss Duncan?" the surgeon asked.

"Fine," Laura answered, wondering if any of the students really knew who Francesco Vinci really was. Had any of them ever heard about John Gravani from Brooklyn?

"Is there something you would like to tell the students, from the point of view of the patient?" Vinci asked again.

Laura thought for a moment. She had not expected such a curious beginning. It seemed show business in the operating room. However, she had the feeling Vinci wanted the audience's praise.

"I just want to say I am very confident in my doctor," she said.

"I am glad to hear that," Vinci answered. He looked at one of his sides. There was the nurse, the anaesthetist.

*   *

"Martha Lawrence's accident was a real tragedy," the administrator of the bowling centre to the lieutenant. "She was severely injured."

The last name of the administrator was Cohen and he was a little and hairy faced man. He was wearing extravagant clothes. While he talked, a big Cuban cigar was hanging from his lips.

"How severe were her injuries, Mister Cohen?" Roth answered.

"She was left disfigured, do you get me? She had to go to a specialist, a plastic surgeon that reconstructed her face."

"Roth nodded. He took Laura's photograph from one of his pockets, but before he showed it to the man, he asked:

"Did you see Martha's face after the surgery?"

"No, detective," Cohen answered. "After the accident and the surgery she never came back to the Bowling again. The only thing I know was that her entire face was reconstructed."

"So you never saw Martha Lawrence again?" Smith intervened in the conversation.

"No… not until they discovered her dead body."

"What did you knew about her? Where did she live? Who were her friends?"

"There isn't much I can tell you about her," Cohen took the Cuban cigar out of his mouth. "Martha was a lonely young woman. She came from a town to the east of Texas; Odessa… I remember I saw her with a guy a couple of times; a former police officer. He gave the name of a person and the address of a bar at the end of Elm Street.

It was twenty past seven in the evening, when Roth and Smith arrived to that bar.

"Good evening," Roth said and gave his name and showed his police badge to the barman. "Do you know Hank Quinlan? WE have heard he comes here once in a while."

"Yes…," the barman answered uninterestedly. He pointed to one of the tables in the back of the bar. There was a man sitting at one of the tables drinking. He was around forty years old and was wearing a cowboy hat.

"The lieutenant and the sergeant walked through the empty tables.

"Mister Quinlan?" Roth asked.

"That is me…" the cowboy turned his head towards them. He was drunk.

Roth sat at the table. Smith did not. The both identified themselves and showed their badges. Roth asked the cowboy, whether they could ask him a few questions related to the murder case of Martha Lawrence. The man nodded.

"What do you want to know about Martha Lawrence, detective...?" The words came slowly out of his mouth.

"She had some kind of accident at home," Roth started to say. "And because of this, Martha underwent a plastic surgery on her face, Am I right, Mister Quinlan?"

"That is right."

"Did you see her after the surgery?"

The cowboy yawned and nodded. Roth took Laura's photograph out of his pocket and showed it to Quinlan.

"That is her," the cowboy answered. "That is Martha..."

Roth left the photograph on the table.

"What can you tell me about her?"

"We went out a couple of times. She was a lonely young woman. She did not have many friends and relatives. After that accident that disfigured her, she became terribly depressed and even lonelier... Thank God she had that surgery that reconstructed her face and gave her back will to live..." the man finished his glass and said disappointedly. "It was a shame she went through a hard time because of it as well!"

"What do you mean by that?"

The cowboy asked Roth for another drink. The lieutenant called the waiter.

"At the beginning Martha's face was unbelievable," Quinlan said. "It was fine and delicate. It wasn't actually her original face, but it was a splendid face... But then something weird happened... The skin started to get loose, scares started to appear... The beauty of the new face became a horrible mask made out of cut flesh...I do not know what could have happened. I guess there was some kind of medical negligence. The waiter brought another glass of whisky. The cowboy drank it. He wiped his mouth with the back of his hand and continued talking. "After that, Martha became very deeply depressed. And then she simply disappeared. Nobody knew anything about her, until they found her dead body...without her head. She was identified though her fingerprints."

"What do you know about the doctor that performed plastic surgery on her?" Roth asked.

"I think he was a renowned surgeon, top class."

"Was the name of that surgeon Vinci, Francesco Vinci?"

"I do not remember, detective."

Roth thought for a moment.

"Do you have any idea of someone that could have killed her?"

"No," the cowboy shook his head. "The Dallas Police asked me that same questions many times. They have no clue of who could have done that to Martha... I, for one thing, as a former policeman, have also done some research of the case, but I have no positive results" He leaned back on the chair he was sitting on and looked at the photograph again. "It was a tragedy. She looks so happy here..."

"The only thing is that she is not Martha Lawrence," Roth answered.

"What?" Quinlan said surprised.

"It does not matter. Look, my friend, Thanks a lot. You were of great help.

*   *

Vinci was already at the last stage of Laura's surgery, in the presence of more or less 50 medicine students. The surgery performed on Laura's left cheek was going to be successful.

"A great part of plastic surgery was not permanent," Vinci told his audience. "People change. Faces change.

Nature is so powerful that it can undo everything that man has sculpted... This is why mistakes are so incredibly disastrous in the field of surgery. The fewer mistakes we commit during a surgery the more successful we will be... In other words, we must be able to achieve perfection in all of our surgeries." He stopped talking for a moment. "Now, we are going to clean all the imperfections," he said to another nurse. "Turn on the laser."

The nurse obeyed. Vinci drank a glass of water. He carefully looked at Laura, and thought he was going to send her a beautiful crown of flowers, decorated with tulips and orchids, to the funeral of that nosy bitch not to be suspicious. He decided to stop thinking about that and concentrated again on the surgery. He told the audience:

"One has to use the laser all the time that it is necessary to erase even the smallest imperfections on the sculpted skin." He raised his voice. "Remember that the highest aspiration of a plastic surgeon is always to find perfection... To achieve this, there needs to be continuous, persistent and precise practice. This is art and we are artists... and the final result of our work has to be similar to a piece of art." He looked at his Cartier golden watch. He realised that it was time to conclude everything. "The last thing I have to say to you, ladies and gentlemen, is that you can never neglect the psychological help a patient, who has undergone plastic surgery, needs to receive." He stroke Laura's face. "My dear friend Laura Duncan, here has received the best help from the best psychiatrist in the state; the prestigious Doctor Alan Jung." He stopped talking for a moment waiting for the audience's applause.

It came immediately.

Laura who had just been under local anaesthesia, carefully listened to Vinci. This man was an expert liar. He seemed trustworthy and respectful. None of the people that were present, except for Laura, would ever suspect that behind that appearance of respectfulness there was a perverse man with the power of a surgical knife.

Vinci ordered one of his assistants:

"Now, nurse, please prepare the magnesium and adenoxine injection, please."

*   *

Lieutenant Sam Roth got out of the taxi and went into the Dallas airport, where he would take a plane back to Miami. He phoned the Miami Globe. A few moments later he was talking to Larry Wallace.

"Hello Sam," Wallace greeted him. "What did you discover about the girl in Dallas?"

Roth cleared his throat before he started talking. After that he told all the details to Wallace, who listened carefully and did not interrupt Roth. The lieutenant stopped talking and Wallace said:

"I will tell all of this to Laura immediately. Maybe she is already back in her room. She will get anxious when I tell there is another murder in this case." He stopped talking for a moment. "Do you know something, Sam?... At the beginning, I did not believe her. I thought she was imagining things or that she maybe was depressed. She does not like doctors and hospitals very much. Her younger sister died in a hospital due to a medical negligence. They gave her the wrong sedative... But I realise now, that there really is something criminal going on around this one man..."

"Francesco Vinci," Roth interrupted him. "He is the centre of everything; he and his clinic... I am sure now too... this man killed them all."

"How can you be so sure?"

"Because of a simple reason," the lieutenant answered. "Those people with the identical face must have meant a lot to him. The most logical thing was that he stayed in contact with them. If one of them disappeared or died, he would have reacted in some way. Maybe he would have expressed his worries in the newspapers. Or he would have gone to the police... But he did not, he just remained behind his elegant desk of his prestigious clinic. He did not give a damn about them, man. Do you realise this?"

Wallace nodded for a moment.

"Yes," he said. "I think you are right.

The syringe full of poison was empty quickly. Nurse Anderson removed the syringe from Laura's arm.

"The injection is ready, doctor," she said to Vinci.

The great plastic surgeon smiled. His hand, which looked like a thin and pale dead man's hand, stroke Laura's head one more time. He told his students: "This injection will help the scar process." He turned to another nurse and ordered her to take the patient to her bedroom so that she could rest.

Laura Duncan, who would start agonizing in less then two hours, was taken out of the operating room.

The fabulous human flesh artist received another wave of applause and ovations in the operating room.

*   *

19

Once she arrived back to her room, Laura felt the local anaesthesia, was fading and her drowsiness as well. She did not feel any kind of pain. Nurse Anderson came to see her and brought her another set of pills Laura had to take in before she left the clinic.

Half an hour after Anderson had left the room, the phone on the night table rang. She fixedly looked at the phone. Everything around her still seemed very foggy and unclear. She reached for the telephone. It seemed her hand took for ages to grab the phone. She finally could grab the phone and could gently put it against her ear.

"Laura?"

She smiled. She had been waiting for Larry Wallace's car.

"Hello, Larry."

"Did you survive the devil with his surgical knife, honey?" Wallace joked.

"This is not a good time to joke around, Larry."

"That is true. I just hope they did not change your face again. I would not bear having met three different women in less than a year."

"I actually do not know how I look like," Laura replied. "They have not given a mirror yet."

"Do you want to hear everything Sam Roth discovered in Dallas?"

"Of course, I do."

"Listen," Wallace hesitated and pressed his teeth. He did not really know if he wanted to tell her the tragic news. It was too depressing. But he had to. Laura wanted to know the truth very much and she was the most interested to make justice in this whole case. He continued: "Well, Roth found another identical face to yours, honey... The young woman's name was Martha Lawrence, she was a waitress..."

"And?"

"She was murdered... She was decapitated, just the way the girl from Las Vegas was."

"Both of them were. We already kind of expected this, didn't we, Larry?"

"Yes, you are right, honey. We did."

"What does Roth think about all of this?"

"He is convinced that Vinci killed them... and the lieutenant had an idea. He thinks that we should go to New Orleans and try to talk to the travesty dancer Scylla Dubois. Roth wants to why, she together with you are still alive. The lieutenant also says that Scylla could be an excellent witness in a murder case against Vinci. What do you think about his proposal?"

"I think it is a good idea."

"On the other hand, the lieutenant mentioned he was afraid of your safety, Laura," Wallace added to the conversation. "He thinks that Vinci could try and harm you... You are alive after the surgery at least.

Laura was silent for a moment.

"Like I already told you Larry, he does not do anything in his clinic."

"Anyway, Roth will send a policewoman to the clinic. This policewoman will wear a nurse uniform. Nobody in Vinci's clinic will be suspicious of her. You just have to tell the doctor and his employees that she is a private nurse you hired. Would you do that honey? The policewoman will soon be over there."

"All right," Laura answered.

"When will you be sent home?"

"After four o'clock in the afternoon."

"I will come around to see you when you are home." Then Wallace hung up.

Laura hung up the phone, while she felt very tired. She also felt relieved that Roth was now interested in the case.

However, there was still a big obstacle; all of the evidence against Vinci was not so strong. What concrete evidence was there that proofed that he had killed those other two patients with identical faces? And where was the weapon that could link him to those two murders?

Someone knocked on the door. After that, Laura's worst nightmare could ever had had in her twenty eight years of life.

"Hello Miss Duncan," Vinci voice said as delicately as the first she had ever heard it. "How are you doing?"

"Well, doctor... very well," Laura answered.

Vinci suddenly felt extremely angry as he realised that Laura seemed not to be experiencing any effect of the mortal poison. What was happening to the bitch? In spite the fact that he was enraged; the great surgeon looked completely serene and calm on the outside.

"Are you are you are feeling al right, Miss Duncan?" he asked again.

"Yes, doctor. Why do you ask?"

"Just because. I am just checking how you are doing after the surgery, like I do with any of my patients."

Laura did not say anything else. Vinci looked at his Cartier. '*It had been already an hour from the injection...and Laura was not showing any signs of agony. What the hell was going on? Why was Laura Duncan not feeling weak?*'

Vinci rage became bigger and stronger. He decided to leave the room and not explode in anger right in front of Laura. He told her he had to make his round at the clinic and visit some other patients.

*   *

At a quarter past four in the afternoon, Francesco Vinci, feeling blinded by rage, was astonished to see Laura Duncan was leaving the clinic on her own feet. And she looked as fresh and radiant as a lettuce.

The doctor was confused and annoyed. *'How was it possible that she was still alive? Why had the poison not worked? Maybe something went wrong. But what?'*

Half an hour later he had the answer to everything. And it came from the mouth of the dedicated and competent nurse Anderson:

"Doctor, I have to inform you that the renewal of the medicine in the cabinet in the cellar has been done early this time."

Vinci could not believe what he was hearing. As clinic regulation, all the medicine in the cellar had to be replaced periodically. To be exact; every three months. They have to be replaced by other that have a more recent expiring date. And one of the people, Vinci had trusted to do this task was precisely nurse Anderson; she had the key to the cabinet and also knew how to deactivate the alarms.

"But... But there are still two weeks left for the next renewal date," Vinci mumbled completely disappointed. "Why did you do it, nurse?"

"I took the freedom to do it, doctor," Anderson started to apologise. "After the patient Laura Duncan was a bit reluctant to take the pills I gave her... I hope you take this the wrong way. I thought it was the best thing to do."

"The nurse's words were so honest and calm, that Vinci did not know whether to be angry at her or congratulate for her efficiency. Vinci swallowed and decided to control himself. Then he told her:

"Please, leave me alone..."

Anderson left immediately and noticed, by the tone of the surgeon's voice, he was annoyed because of something. The nurse did not really understand why he could be annoyed. She only knew that when Vinci asked to be alone, the best thing to do was to get out of his sight.

Anderson left the office, closing the door behind her.

Vinci felt beaten and defeated, just like a boxer after loosing a one round... but he had not lost the final battle yet. He sat at his desk and opened one of his drawers. He inhaled some cocaine he took from inside it. H was getting too accustomed to that dust he thought. If he went on like that, he would end up being an addict. That was dangerous; his body could end up rotten, before he had a change to make his dreams come true.

He closed his eyes, and though he had failed at his first attempt to kill Laura Duncan; it had been the only failed murder in his career...

She could escape Francesco Vinci, but she would not be able to escape John Gravani.

He would try again. Soon.

He had to kill that ungrateful bitch; he would crush her like a cockroach. He had not other option.

*   *

20

The twenty eight year old woman Vinci was planning to crush was also planning her next move. The morning after she had left the great surgeon's clinic, she was on board of an American Airlines plane flying to New Orleans with Larry Wallace and Sam Roth. The three of them were planning to contact Scylla Dubois and convince him to reveal all the information he knew about Vinci and his experiment with identical faces.

Larry and Laura had paid their on tourist class tickets of course. On the other hand, the Miami Police department had paid for the Lieutenant's ticket. Just when the Boeing was crossing the sky of the Golf of Mexico, Roth leaned over and said something about his strategy to catch Vinci:

"The first thing we have to do is to show that the plastic surgeon was not in Miami at the time the murders, we know about, were committed. The second thing we have to do is to prove he was in Las Vegas and Dallas on the exact dates of the murders; although this is not very convincing evidence."

"Why not?" Laura asked.

"Vinci does not have to make all his business public. You can arrive and leave Las Vegas very fast and leave no evidence behind. You can change your appearance; take taxis instead of renting a car and having to leave your credit car number. You can avoid going to places where people can recognise you. I really think Vinci travelled to these two cities to kill these women, but I also think nobody knew where he was... There is also a change he send someone to kill those women; this means another person did the dirty job for him..."

"What you are telling us is not very encouraging, lieutenant," Laura said. "What do we have left then?"

"What we have left, is everything we can do together. Maybe Scylla Dubois, that homosexual dancer from New Orleans, can help us more then we expect... Actually, at this point, that homosexual dancer is our best shot at knowing the truth."

"All right, we have to talk to Scylla. She will probably ask for money before she tells us everything she knows."

"I do not think so," Roth answered. "Once she realises I am a policeman, she will become as docile as a lamb. She will spit everything out. I can assure you that, Miss Duncan."

"I see," Laura said. After that she meditated a little. "But, what will happen, if what she knows is not relevant enough to catch Vinci."

"In that case," Roth answered, "we will have to work even harder. Total investigation. Directly confront Vinci. Call each and every one of his employees. Obviously, the plastic surgeon will have foreseen a situation like this. But maybe we will have to do this. The problem will be that it will affect his reputation... That can be a serious matter."

"Why?"

"Because of his lawyers," Larry Wallace intervened. "If it damages his reputation and he is innocent, he will come after us. It will be his vengeance."

Laura listened to Larry's words. She began to feel extremely angry. The anger started bottling up and finally became rage. If Vinci could get away because of legal tramps, that would be very unjust. Even more, if he could sue them and become even richer."

Laura thought of poor Mister Bardin looking for his missing daughter. Then she remembered the two decapitated bodies. How many other victims were there...? She thought about her own face. She thought about the fact that Vinci had made her part of his plan. A very perverse and sinister plan. If she had not met Nora's father, the matter would have never been revealed... And Vinci would have gone on deceiving people... but the world was not made for dishonest people as him; his cruelty, his fraud and his evil indifference had to be punished.

"I will catch him," Laura raised her voice.

Wallace and Roth looked at each other surprised.

"I will only rest after I catch him," she added.

*   *

A damp heat surrounded the city of New Orleans as a blanket.

Laura, Wallace and Roth got off the taxi and went down an alley that was perpendicular to the Jackson Square in the French Quarter.

They arrived at an old wooden house that had three floors. That was the place were Scylla Dubois lived. The three of them went up the old stairs, which stank. Finally they arrived at the travesty's room.

Laura knocked on the plain door. The three of them waited. There was no answer.

"Is there anybody home?" Laura asked then.

There was silence.

She looked at her watch. It was just a few minutes past noon. Then Roth and Wallace knocked at the door again. The lit some cigarettes and waited. A few minutes went by and nothing happened. Nothing. "Maybe our friend went shopping," Wallace mumbled. He pointed at the door and made a gesture to the lieutenant. "What do you say, Sam? Would you be able to knock it down?"

"No," Roth answered and shook his head. "I have no authority here in Louisiana. I need a warrant. The boys at the New Orleans Police Department will have to do the job."

The three of them decide to wait twenty more minutes. But nobody came out of or entered Scylla's room.

"I will call the club where she works," Laura said. She walked back to the hall where there was a public phone.

Roth and Wallace waited next to the door. They lit another pair of cigarettes.

Five minutes went by and Laura returned to her friends. He face was as pale as paper.

"What is wrong, honey?" Wallace asked her.

"I... I called the Magnolia Club where Scylla danced," Laura mumbled. "She has disappeared without leaving any trace. She did not turn up for work last night. Nobody knows where she is...." She stopped talking for a moment. "But her car has been found abandoned near Lake Pontchartrain. The police are investigating the case."

Roth though for a moment; and then he said:

"I bet that disappearance has something to do with a certain plastic surgeon we all know..."

"Do you think Francesco Vinci...?" Laura whispered.

"Yes, I do," Roth answered, as he felt his throat getting dry. He needed a drink. But not yet; he had to find out something first. He told Laura and Larry: "Scylla disappears just at the moment we are investigating Vinci." Roth wiped his sweaty with a handkerchief. Then he said: "I think the time has come to meet my colleagues from New Orleans. I have to find out about this disappearance."

*   *

"Scylla disappeared last night," inspector Laveaux said. He was in charge of the homicide Department of the Police of that Town. "The missing report was filed by the owners of the magnolia nightclub. We have already started looking for her. There is a change that this is a murder case and that the body is in the bottom of the lake.

"What makes you so sure?" Roth asked.

"We found some blood stains at the front part of the Volkswagen that was abandoned by the lake. It was property of the homosexual dancer. The blood stains on the pier indicate that Scylla was dragged to the edge of the lake... Six divers of the Police department are looking through the area."

"How long will it take them to find the body?" Roth asked.

"I do not know. The Pontchartrain is very big and it has some low water currents... maybe the body was moved to another place in the lake by one of these currents."

Roth though that the search of a body in that lake could easily take weeks of even months before finding it... He was disappointed. He looked through the window of Laveaux's office and saw Larry and Laura waiting in the hall. He had to tell them the bad news he had received from the inspector.

Roth went out of the office. He lit a cigarette and walked toward his friends from Miami. He started telling them the news.

Before he finished a detective stormed into Laveaux's office...

A short while after that, the inspector from Louisiana called Roth. Laveaux's face was shining:

"We have been very lucky, lieutenant," he said to Roth. "We have found the dancer's body." He immediately started to explain the way the police divers had found and rescued the body of Scylla Dubois.

*   *

"The body is complete," Roth mentioned to Inspector Laveaux.

Both detectives and the police divers were standing on the muddy shore of the Pontchartrain, and they were looking at a naked body of a man. The water had done some damage anyway. The body was swollen because of the gasses inside it. It was clearly in a clear state of decomposition. It was not a nice scene to watch... Although the body had its head, its face was completely disfigured by the multiple stabs it had received... There were so many cuts in the face that it was hard to identify the victim. The eyes had been cut out. It was evident that somebody had vented his anger on that face.

Laveaux told Roth that one of the employers of the Magnolia Club, who had known Scylla very well, had been called to the place of the discovery and had immediately recognised it was the dancer's body.

Laveaux turned the body over with his feet. The murderer had stuck a cypress stick in the victim's anus.

Roth silently looked at the body. He was not surprised about the disfigured face, or about the cypress stick. It was not the first time he saw a homosexual that had been killed in that way. He sensed who could be behind the murder. However he needed concrete evidence to be able to proof it. He asked Laveaux:

"I suppose you will be in charge of this case?"

"Yes," answered the inspector. "It happened in my territory."

Roth felt a bit annoyed. He knew he could not stick his nose in another police officer's territory. So he had to leave everything in the hands of Laveaux and his people, without being able to hurry things up. In spite of this, he asked the inspector:

"Could you please keep me informed of the progress of this investigation?"

Laveaux nodded. Roth gave him his office number at the Miami Police Department. Then he stepped away from the body and walked towards one of the police cars of the New Orleans sleuth. Laura and Larry were waiting for him in the car. The lieutenant explained the condition that Scylla's body had been found to both of them.

The three of them returned to Florida that same night.

21

Long before his trip to Louisiana, Sam Roth had decided he would go and talk to Francesco Vinci. Sometimes the best way to get answers was to go and talk to enemy personally. He was not daunted by the influences and the prestige of the great plastic surgeon. He knew that police officers had a certain special status; it was like a spell, an aura of adventure and above all the power to arrest. This was something that gave them a certain importance which was not reflected by thick check books or the brand of the car.

Roth had to wait in the reception of Vinci's clinic for about twenty minutes. He looked at the secretaries and nurses' legs, before the great surgeon agreed on receiving him.

"Please sit down, Lieutenant Roth," Vinci's fine and arrogant voice. "I hope that this is not something too serious."

Roth did not sit down. He always preferred to stand in front of someone he had to question. He said:

"Well, it is actually very serious, doctor. It is a sad and tragic matter."

Vinci looked fixedly at the lieutenant. He wrinkled his forehead. He took a deep breath and wondered what this police man really knew.

"I am all ears, lieutenant."

"Well," Roth nodded. "Can I ask you some questions, then?"

"Of course," Vinci smiled nervously. "Ask whatever you want. Are you sure you do not want to sit down?"

Roth shook his head. He though for a moment and then continued:

"Doctor, you must be aware that we are in contact with a lot of cities."

"I guess you are," Vinci said. His heart started to beat very hard in his chest.

"And do you know something else?" Roth clenched the muscles of his yaw. "We have some news that can disturb you..."

Vinci waited for a while before he answered:

"Is it about... the girl in Kansas?" he hesitated. "The one that disappeared...?"

"Among other people," the lieutenant answered.

"What do you mean?"

"Doctor, three of your patients have been murdered. Two women and one man..."

Vinci seemed confused and swallowed heavily.

"Are you kidding, lieutenant?"

"I do not joke around when I am talking about dead bodies," Roth answered. "Especially not when we are talking about two decapitated women and a man with a disfigured face."

Vinci's trembling hand went though his dark hair. His eyes were almost jumping out of his face.

"I had no idea about what you are saying..."

"I thought you knew," Roth said surprised. "Don't doctors stay in touch with their patients?"

"Sometimes," Vinci answered. "Look, detective... What you are saying is terrible. But you have not told who these women and man are. And why have they been murdered?" He was pretending to be surprised. "My patients!"

"Those women and that man," Roth continued saying, "looked very similar."

"What do you mean they looked very similar?" Vinci was incredible histrionic. He did not answer for a long moment. He swallowed again and finally said: "Oh my God!... The experiment... Now I understand who you are talking about... God! The three of them? Of course I know who they are. Why didn't anyone contact me? They should have…"

"Well, doctor," Roth said, "I want you to know that you are not a suspect."

"Lieutenant, do you know what? That is not important now. What worries me are my patients!"

"I see," the detective said. "I wonder why you did not know about these murders… You mentioned something about an experiment. Can you explain that to me?"

"It was a facial plastic surgery experiment. Something really groundbreaking." Vinci answered. He faked his concern. "The two women and the man had that in common: the same face reconstruction performed by me. Yes, it was a wonderful experiment… But if they have been murdered; then it is not a coincidence. What do you think?"

"Of course it is not a coincidence;" the lieutenant replied.

"So, who is responsible for them? Why is there not an investigation going on?"

"That is what I am doing, doctor," Roth answered. "I think its is possible that someone is trying to harm you through your patients." He stopped talking for a moment. "One of the reasons I came here, was to ask you a record of all the people that have worked here and also of all your patients for the last five years. Could you give me that information?"

"Yes, lieutenant. I will happily give that to you. I will send the information to your office in the Police Department."

Roth nodded. Then he asked:

"By the way, do you have another patient with a similar face as the three victims?"

"Yes," Vinci answered. He had to be careful; otherwise this cop would suspect something. "Her name is Laura Duncan. She is a well-known pianist and lives here in Miami. She is a wonderful person… God! She has to be protected!"

Roth nodded.

"We will take of that, doctor."

A second later, the great surgeon regretted he said that. He reproached himself. The last thing he wanted was that that ungrateful bitch received police protection. The intercom rang loudly. It was Vinci's secretary. He previously had told her to call after a certain time to end the meeting with the detective. The surgeon said some monosyllables to the nurse and then he hung up. He told Roth:

"I am sorry to end our chat, lieutenant, but I have to go to the operating room. One of my patients, that had been recently been operated, has suffered a nervous attack, because she is not happy with her new face... This is something normal in some women that undergo plastic surgery."

"I understand," Roth said. He also though that it was time to get the hell away from that elegant and tricky clinic. "Alright, doctor, I won't waste anymore of your time. I know you are a very busy person."

As soon as the lieutenant had left the room, Vinci felt difficulty breathing. He felt asphyxiated by the feeling of a near end. John Gravani's, the poor boy from Brooklyn, chaotic ghost appeared in his life again. The jealous and mean world wanted to destroy him once more. Again, people wanted to put a rope around the young John Gravani's neck, who now was a prestigious surgeon.

He hated cops... The same way he hated poverty and failure...

He concluded that those bloodhounds were all over him because that fucking Laura Duncan must have contacted them. But he would end those contacts... He would kill the dammed pianist as soon as possible.

How would he be able to do that without being suspicious? He did not really know how, however it was essential she disappeared from the face of the earth.

*　　*

The lieutenant was confused when he left the great surgeon's office. On one side, he was undoubtedly a strange person; Larry had told Roth Vinci's turbulent past. But on the other side, the doctor was capable of feeling really concerned about the homicide of three of his patients. He also seemed worried about Laura. Although, it all could have been a good act. The great performer. It was very possible, that Vinci hid his emotions and his intentions... the same way he hid his past.

Roth felt that the next thing he should do, was to protect the woman that had received the same face as the three murder victims.

He would also put the great surgeon under surveillance.

22

That night, once again Vinci could not sleep. And all because of that bitch! Finally, when it was already dawn, he decided to get out of bed and to go to the living room. With the help of a glass of whisky and some grams of cocaine to clear his head, he planned how he would get rid of Laura.

At five thirty in the morning he already had an idea about it.

He picked up his telephone and dialled a number.

On the other end of the line, the telephone rang several times before someone answered.

"Francesco? Is that you...?" Alan Jung answered sleepy.

Vinci smiled as he recognised the psychiatrist's frightened voice. Piece of chicken shit!

"Yes, Alan," Vinci answered. "It is me."

"What... What do you want? Why are you calling at this time?"

Vinci smiled again. He did not talk for a second. Then he said:

"I need a favour from you, my friend. It is a matter of life or dead... It has to do with that bitch... she thinks she can finish us of..."

"Are you talking about Laura... Laura Duncan?"

"Of course I am talking about her," the surgeon groaned.

At the other side of the telephone, the psychiatrist woke up completely. He sat straight in his bed and he wished he could stay away from Vinci. Although he knew it was too late for that. He had been an accomplice of the atrocious surgical experiments of that brilliant though contaminated mind. In a certain way, he and Vinci were connected through a kind of corrupted umbilical cord until the end. Jung did not say a word for a moment and then he asked:

"I am listening to you, Francesco...."

*   *

It was around seven o'clock in the morning and the sun was already heating the south of the states of Florida.

Laura Duncan, who had become Vinci obsession, was still asleep when the telephone in her room started ringing. Laura woke up slowly. She opened her eyes and yawned. She slowly moved in her bed. She grabbed the telephone on the night table and put it next to her ear.

"Miss Duncan? It is me, Doctor Jung."

"Oh... How are you, doctor?" Laura answered a little surprised of hearing the psychiatrist and still feeling very sleepy.

On the other side of the line there was silence.

"Laura..." Jung mumbled. "I am calling because of something..." his voice was hardly coming out of his mouth.

"What is wrong, doctor?"

"It is something," Jung continued; "related to the things you told me some days ago... about Doctor Francesco Vinci and his weird professional behaviour..."

Laura felt oppression in her chest.

"What is it, doctor?"

"It is actually too important to talk about it over the phone. But I will explain it very briefly. Some days ago, I got into one of Vinci's computers... and I discovered some things..."

"What did you discover?"

"It some related ton the experiment about the identical faces. But as I already told you, I would prefer to talk to you personally about what I discovered. After that you can decide if you want to go to the police with the information... I have to protect my reputation, and I would prefer to stay away from everything." He stopped talking for a moment. "That is why I am calling you. I want to know if you could come to my office this morning. Let's say at nine o'clock..."

Laura's heart started beating very fast. She thought that maybe Vinci's computer could have the evidence that Roth and his men needed to press charges against the surgeon with multiple murder... Laura did not feel suspicious of the psychiatrist's words. He had promised confidentiality to her. At least this is what the naive girl thought. She did not even suspect that Jung was the monster's accomplice. This is why she did not doubt to accept the invitation for a minute.

"All right, doctor," Laura said. "I will be in your office around nine o'clock."

"Fair enough," Jung said. He hesitated for an instant and then added: "Laura, first I want to ask you something..."

"What, doctor?"

Laura could barely hear Jung's voice.

"Could you please not mention our meeting to anyone? Absolutely anyone. As I mentioned to you before, I do not wish to see my name mentioned in this embarrassing situation later on. Something like this would surely destroy my professional career. Do you understand what I am saying?"

"Perfectly well, doctor," Laura said. "Nobody will know about our meeting."

"Thank you," Jung said. And then he hung up.

23

Vinci's elegant Lamborghini stopped in an alley in Twenty Four Street. The surgeon opened the door of his car and got out. He put on his dark sunglasses and nervously lit a cigarette.

He started to walk, because he knew he had to walk about five streets until Bsicayne Boulevard, where Alan Jung's office.

He walked anxiously while he released mouthfuls of smoke. The heat in the morning was suffocating. He soon started to sweat. His hands, his chest, and his armpits were soaked in cold sweat. He took of his fine and white elegant jacket and put it under his left arm.

What the distinguished doctor did not know was that two undercover police officers, dressed as simple tourists spending some days in Miami enjoying the sun and the beaches, were following him.

Twenty minutes later, when Vinci arrived at the psychiatrist's office, the two police officers that were following him, waited on the corner. A black car picked them up. The two fake police officers, between jokes, they completed the records about the movements of the surgeon.

Alan Jung opened the door of the office before Vinci pressed the bell.

"Come in, Francesco," he mumbled. He stepped out of the threshold.

Vinci stormed in the room, without saying anything and letting his head hang down.

"Sit down, my friend," Jung said and pointed at the sofa.

"I would prefer to stand...," Vinci answered. He left his jacket on the sofa. He fixed his eyes on the psychiatrist. "Did you do what I asked you to?"

"Of course," Jung answered. "Laura Duncan does not suspect anything. She accepted to meet me, without any problem." He looked at his watch. "She will be here in... exactly an hour."

"I am glad to hear this," Vinci whispered, wondering if Jung suspected that these hours were going to be his last. The same as for that bitch..."

"Tell me something, Francesco," Jung asked curiously, "Do you think Laura Duncan has taken her investigation to far? I mean, do you think she has enough evidence to destroy our professional careers?"

"I am sure she has," Vinci answered. He told the psychiatrist about Sam Roth's sudden visit to the clinic.

Vinci stopped talking; and Jung said concerned:

"Damned, this seems more serious than I thought. Nor a cop nor a homicide lieutenant had ever gone to your clinic to question you," he whispered and stopped talking. "And what are thinking to do with Laura Duncan when she walks through that door?"

"I will crash her like a bug," Vinci answered. He made a gesture to Jung. "But Alan, where are your modals? Are you going to offer me something a martini or something…?"

"Of course," Jung answered. He walked towards an ebony cupboard. He turned his back on his surgeon and opened the cupboard. "Are you really going to that in my office?"

Vinci did not answer, but he walked towards Jung while he put his surgical gloves on. When the psychiatrist turned around holding the glass of martini in his hands, Vinci already had the sharp surgical in his right hand… He cut Alan Jung's thin throat…

The glass of alcohol flew from the psychiatrist's hands, who as he noticed his life was being attacked tried to react. However he could not…"

Vinci cut Jung's throat deeply. As a surgeon, he knew the most efficient way to cut the carotid and the jugular which would cause the victim to bleed to death.

The moment he was murdering Jung, the great plastic surgeon had the strange impression he was not doing that. No!… He had the impression it was the ghost of the violent John Gravani that had returned from the past to commit another one of his crimes.

The psychiatrist's legs bended. His body fell on the floor. The surgical knife was sticking out of bloody flesh of the throat seemed a horrible physical deformation. He slowly stopped breathing… and then he died.

After that Vinci dragged the dead body to the bathroom, trying to avoid the blood, which was still pouring out of Jung's throat, stained the carpet too much. He did not want Laura to immediately find out that a crime was committed in that place the moment she arrived. He did not want her to run away scared.

Then he took out the surgical knife out of Jung's throat and cleaned it with the psychiatrist's clothes. He wrapped the knife in a handkerchief and put it back into the pocket of his trousers. Then, he took of the surgical gloves stained with blood; he threw it into toilet and flushed it. He closed the door of the bathroom.

He opened the drawers of the desk, the filing cabinet and the cupboards. He went through everything. He wanted to give the idea that the place had been robbed by thieves...

He finally said down on a chair next to the door. He looked at his golden Cartier. He still had half an hour until the bitch would arrive.

He wiped the sweat of his forehead and inhaled a finger full of cocaine to feel clear headed.

*   *

Laura put on a flowery coloured silk dress and brushed his long brown hair in front of the mirror.

She drank a cup of coffee while she analyzed Doctor Jung's phone call. In spite of the fact she fully trust in that serene and kind man, she thought the hour of the meeting seemed a bit unusual to her. It was evidently urgent. What had the psychiatrist found that involved Vinci in the murderers?

She would know soon.

She considered the idea of calling Wallace and tell him about the sudden meeting with the psychiatrist. She hesitated. But she immediately remembered Jung's request. So she did not.

She finished her coffee. She was so curious of knowing what she would find in the psychiatrist's office that she grabbed he fine bag and left the house.

It took about ten minutes to arrive to the office. Laura was driven by the young and athletic agent Fitzpatrick, who was the detective chosen by Roth to look after her.

The car stopped in front of the beautiful entrance. It had roman columns made out of marble.

"Would you like me to wait for you, Miss Duncan?" the detective asked Laura.

"It is not necessary," she answered. She looked at her watch. "Do you know what, detective? Why don't you go and have breakfast near here? Then you can come back for me; in half an hour. What do you think?"

Fitzpatrick doubted for a second and said:

"I am not used to loosing the people under my attention. But at least tell me who it is."

"It is just my psychiatrist, Alan Jung," Laura said. "There is nothing to worry about. He is a charming person."

The detective thought Laura's proposal over a bit longer. He finally accepted and made a gesture. He started the engine of the car.

Laura looked at the vehicle until it disappeared from her eyesight.

She opened the iron gate and went up the stone stairs. She walked towards the psychiatrist's office.

24

Twenty minutes after Sam Roth had arrived at his office in the Homicide Brigade, the telephone rang. It was a call from Louisiana. Inspector Laveaux had some information related to the murder of Scylla Dubois.

While Roth absorbed the details from New Orleans, his hard face was filled with surprise. The conversation with Laveaux was brief, it did not last more than a few minutes. Then Roth grabbed the phone and dialled Laura Duncan's telephone number, thinking he would give her the good news.

Nobody answered the phone. Roth patiently waited, but nothing happened.

He thought that the attractive young woman maybe had gone to Larry Wallace's house. It was obvious there was something more going on between those two beside a simple friendship.

He now dialled the number of the house of the journalist of the Miami Globe.

"Sam," Wallace answered. "How are you?"

"Hello," the lieutenant said. "I was just calling to know if Laura was there with you."

"She is not here," Wallace answered. "She must be at home."

"Laura is not there, man. Her phone does not answer."

"Why do you want to talk to her?"

"I have some good news from new Orleans. Inspector Laveaux called me this morning. They have found a witness; a taxi driver, who has identified a passenger that asked him to be driven to the area of the pier on Lake Pontchartrain on the same night Dubois was killed. The driver gave the description of the passenger. It is a young and elegant man, wearing a golden Cartier on his left wrist and a diamond in his tie."

"That is him. That is Vinci," Wallace replied.

"I also think it is Vinci," said the lieutenant. "This is what I wanted to tell Laura, but she is not at home...that is a bit strange don't you think?"

Wallace started to get a bit nervous. He though fast and asked:

"And what about the detective that is watching after her?"

"Of course. How could I have forgotten...? I will talk to agent Fitzpatrick; he must know where Laura is."

"After you talk with the agent," Wallace told him, "please call me back. I guess I am a bit worried about Laura."

"I will," Roth hung up.

Less than three minutes later, Wallace heard the lieutenant's voice again:

"Larry, the agent says that she went to her psychiatrist's office on Biscayne Boulevard. His name is Alan Jung. Do you know that doctor?"

"Yes," Wallace answered. "It seemed that it is a trustworthy person." Wallace heard some noise on the other said of the line, some conversation and some paper noise. The homicide lieutenant was talking to someone.

"Larry, are you still there...?" Roth asked upset a instant later.

"Is there something wrong?"

"Damned! I have just received the information that Vinci has gone to the same place... To that psychiatrist's office..."

Wallace on the other side of the line felt shivers run down his spine.

"But, but she, Laura must not have known..." Wallace mumbled. "She would not go there, she would not do such a thing." He stopped talking for a moment ad sighed. "Now that I remember, that psychiatrist was recommended to her by Vinci himself... Both doctors knew each other... God! Maybe it is a set up."

"Damned!" groaned Roth. "I am going to go this psychiatrist's office right away! You do the same thing. Laura may be in danger..."

*   *

The door of the office was slightly open. Laura thought had left the door like that so that she could just go in.

"Doctor Jung?"

Nobody answered. Laura calmly went into the room. She looked around the office. The first thing she saw was that the drawers of the desk were open and that everything inside them had been scattered around on the floor. Something similar had happened with the cupboard. Someone had forced it open and had gone through the things inside it.

Laura wondered what had happened there... She was still trying to find an answer, when she suddenly felt like a powerful claw grabbed her by the back of her neck and pulled her inside the room. She fell on her knees on the carpet. Her heart started to beat frenetically. She immediately looked up:

"Doctor Vinci!"

Francesco Vinci was standing in front of her. He was not wearing a shirt and looked at her in a despicable way. He kicked the door of the office and closed.

"Bitch!" The elegant and educated voice of the surgeon Laura knew was gone.

"But... What are you doing here?" she stammered. "Where is Doctor Jung?"

"Alan will not be able to help you..."

At that moment, Laura saw the blood stains on the carpet and knew straight away what had happened. Still on her knees on the carpet she mumbled:

"Oh my God...You... You killed him, didn't you? You killed Jung..."

Vinci did not answer; he just stepped towards her and furiously grabbed her long hair.

"Stand up, bitch... and look at me," the great surgeon ordered.

She stood up, shaking. Vinci had her hair in a strong grasp, so she hardly could not move.

"Why did you betray me, Laura?...You ungrateful bitch!" he spat out. "I made you beautiful. The woman with the most attractive face someone could ever imagine. But...but you doubted my talent...You investigated me, you went through my things...You discovered the 'experiment'..."

"The police know everything," Laura stammered. "They also know where I am. They will soon come from me..."

Vinci seemed not to be listening to her.

"You disappointed me!" Vinci groaned. After that he slapped on her face. Laura lips started to bleed. Vinci went on: "I was creating the perfect face. The face of the twenty first century... A face that would be immortal... Remembered for centuries and centuries to come... But you screwed it all up." He turned his head and looked at Laura and screamed at her: "you destroyed my great dream, you nosy bitch!"

"You are sick, doctor!" she screamed hysterically. "You are crazy...!"

"That is the same thing they said about Leonardo, Michael Angelo and Vincent van Gogh. They were all great artists..."

"What will you do with me...?" Laura asked terrified.

Vinci slapped her violently again. Now, Laura nose bleed. Immediately blood fell from her nose and dripped down her mouth and her neck.

"Bastard!"

Slowly, at taking al the time to do it, Francesco Vinci, or better said, John Gravani; the poor boy of Brooklyn, son of painter and a cook, took the handkerchief with the surgical knife from his pocket. He held the surgical instrument in his hand while he whispered at her:

"Never again, Laura..."

"Never again what...?"

"Never again," Vinci insisted as he lifted the surgical knife. "You will never be beautiful again... They will not be able to open you coffin. And those who do will throw up... It will be like the old days. Just like after the accident."

Laura's blood froze in her veins. Oh my God! She had to do something before all of that became a horrible massacre. She remembered something she learned as a teenager.

Vinci never expected her to kick him right between the legs. Just at his balls. That bitch!

Vinci groaned of pain. He let go of Laura's hair and at the same time he tried to stab her. She moved backwards and the surgical knife only cut the air, some centimetres in front of her. Laura knew she only had some seconds to counterattack…She saw a bronze lamp on Jung's desk, and without a doubt in her mind, she grabbed it. She turned to the surgeon, lifted the lamp and violently beat her adversary.

The surgeon's face immediately erupted in blood. Then, Laura, possessed by a nervous attack, something that had not happened to her for years, kept on beating Vinci's blooded face one time after another.

"Your face, son of a bitch! It will be your face! I will destroy your face!" Laura shouted desperately, while kept on beating man's face.

Vinci dropped the surgical knife and his knees bended. He fell on the floor. While he fell, she kept on beating his face violently with the lamp.

She was so concentrated in what she was doing, that she did not hear the noise of the door being kicked in.

She did not hear a person come into the office, followed by other people… She just felt some robust and protective arms surround her body confidently and moving her away of the body on the floor of the room.

"Calm down, Laura! Calm down! Stop! Everything is over! Everything is over!" a sharp voice shouted at her.

The lamp covered in blood slipped from Laura's hands and fell on the carpet. She slowly recovered her calmness and her sanity. Her mind cleared. She distinguished Sam Roth who was holding her. Behind him was Larry Wallace, together with a dozen of police officers… She immediately looked at the body on the floor. The face was completely covered in blood and totally disfigured. It seemed like a bloody mask… Vinci had died already…

"Did I do that?" She asked, as she looked disgusted at that deformed face. "How was I able to do something like that?"

As she wondered what she had done, she felt pain in her nose and lips. Vinci had also brutally beaten her. And the red and fresh stains on his hands and her dress were mixed blood; hers and his.

And then, while her heart slowed down its beatings, she understood that she had become a violent and aggressive person for a moment. And all because of that bastard...It seemed strange but she did not feel repentance for the things she had done. She only felt disappointed. In a certain, she had destroyed the disturbed surgeon with the same indifference he had killed his victims.

However, she also understood that the eccentric face creator was also a part of her...Her face had been a present from him; she was just as he had dreamed her to be, beautiful with a splendid face...Paradoxically, beside Vinci's desire to destroy her, he had given her hope and a future...

The monster with the surgical knife would stay with her forever.

THE END